American Night:
The Ballad of Juan José

Richard J. Montoya

A SAMUEL FRENCH ACTING EDITION

FOUNDED 1830

SAMUELFRENCH.COM
SAMUELFRENCH-LONDON.CO.UK

FOR PRODUCTION ENQUIRIES

UNITED STATES AND CANADA
Info@SamuelFrench.com
1-866-598-8449

UNITED KINGDOM AND EUROPE
Plays@SamuelFrench-London.co.uk
020-7255-4302

Each title is subject to availability from Samuel French, depending upon country of performance. Please be aware that *AMERICAN NIGHT: THE BALLAD OF JUAN JOSÉ* may not be licensed by Samuel French in your territory. Professional and amateur producers should contact the nearest Samuel French office or licensing partner to verify availability.

MUSIC USE NOTE

Licensees are solely responsible for obtaining formal written permission from copyright owners to use copyrighted music in the performance of this play and are strongly cautioned to do so. If no such permission is obtained by the licensee, then the licensee must use only original music that the licensee owns and controls. Licensees are solely responsible and liable for all music clearances and shall indemnify the copyright owners of the play(s) and their licensing agent, Samuel French, against any costs, expenses, losses and liabilities arising from the use of music by licensees. Please contact the appropriate music licensing authority in your territory for the rights to any incidental music.

IMPORTANT BILLING AND CREDIT REQUIREMENTS

If you have obtained performance rights to this title, please refer to your licensing agreement for important billing and credit requirements.

AMERICAN NIGHT: THE BALLAD OF JUAN JOSE was originally commissioned by The Oregon Shakespeare Festival for American Revolutions: The United States History Cycle. It was developed by Culture Clash and Jo Bonney. The American Revolutions Director was Alson Carrey.

CHARACTER CHART

1. Juan Jose

2. Marachie Band/Crooked Cop #1/Cuoto/Kyle The Bear/Mexican Man/Hobo 2 (Lefty)/Bob Dylan/Another Man in Audience/ICE/ Man in Turban/Shark/Farm Hand/Juan Corona/Ronnie Burke/ Rabbi

3. Marachie Band/Cooked Cop #2/Border Patrol Officer/Teddy Roosevelt/Dona Tencha/Hobo 1 (Pancho)/Foley Man (mr. Kishi)/ Man In Audience/ICE/Sherrif Joe/Sumo Wrestler/Cuban Radio/ Abelardo (Juan Jose's Father)/Sect Woman 1/Neil Diamante

4. Marachie Band/Lydia/Cuevas/Sakajawea/Riala (Mexican Woman)/ Ralf Lazo/Joan Baez/Young Latina In Audience/ICE

5. Skinny Tie 2/Harry Bridges/Nicholas Trist/Lewis (Explorer 2)/ Man in Robe/Announcer/Madrigal Singer/ICE/Fidel Castro/Abe Lincoln

6. Skinny Tie 1/Johnny/Calvary Officer/Calvary Officer Blanchard/ Asian Man in Audience/ICE/Game Show Host/Sect Woman 3/ West Virginia Coal Miner

7. Ben/Saint Adrian/Padre/Hop Ling/Madrigal Singer/Jackie Robinson/Postal Worker/African American Audinece Member 1/ George Washington/Sect Woman 2/Statue of Liberty

8. Mrs. Finney/Calvary Officer/Clark (Explorer 1)/Woman in Robe/ Cavalry Officer Seguin/Woody (Singer)/Anglo Woman in Audience/ICE/Spokes Model/Shark

9. Viola/Border Patrol Officer/Madrigal Singer/Emit Till/African American Audience Member 2/ICE/Ben Franklin/Celia Cruz

AUTHOR'S NOTE

Yo sets! The US Army Tent is borrowed from The Grapes of Wrath and before actually... We borrow too from the fervor and spirituality of the Revival Tent but for another kind of social justice. The Barracks of Manzanar somehow remind us of our fathers who served and of those we held captive on US soil. Your elderly audience may recognize it. Be sure to build it for them. Or a close approximation there of... Gracias!

American Night: The Ballad For A Nation's Soul...

This Dream is fleeting and front-footed... Prepare.

Juan José is not a sleepy Mexican. Even if he does succumb to his exhaustion. No. He is a hyper time-traveler scaling walls and whole epoch's of US history that most concern him. If we slow we risk stepping into melodrama or sentimentality.

We *soldier on.*

Courageously.

Swiftly.

Paradoxically – our Night knows when to well be still – as a matter of survival – should your horse winey or baby cry, your pursuers could well find you.

We are still – then – judiciously we pounce!

Braver is the actor who recedes back into the shadows with the speed of ghost lightening, aware of the accumulative power of this Night and unconcerned with finding or making too much of the individual moment: a revolutionary action for the collective as storyteller/actor!

Juan José needs this from us most urgently.

Help me prosecute his case.

And allow this Immigrant to dream. Consider that Juan José is not merely a re-actor in his dream. No. At times his words and his actions propel the dream reeling into over-drive.

The Night is here, lo, we must move!

Trampling Rove underfoot and carrying our banned books of Arizona across America.

One...

for mountain lion montoya - two and half years young

(The Stage: A nearly open space.)

(Far upstage resembles box cars or a corrugated steel wall.)

(Razor wire could snake high atop The Wall. [It lights lovely.])

(This text is scrawled in the universal language of graffiti:)

FRONTERAS: Cicatrices en la Tierra...

BORDERS: Scars on the Earth...

(Swirling sounds of Mexican radio and Evangelical static:)

(A man enters – this is **JUAN JOSÉ**.*)*

*(***JUAN JOSÉ*** reaches center stage and steps onto an embedded treadmill where he walks and walks then stops:)*

JUAN JOSÉ. I had to flee my hometown...
Too many guns and bullets that do not miss
My mother had too many tears in her eyes
And too many sons in the ground... So, now...

(Two men have entered: Brother and Elder Clark.)

(They wear white shirts, black ties, name tags and glasses.)

(In a flash, a table and chairs are set in place. lights shift:)

I have it the Green Card. *(holding it up)* Okay. But what this mean? Permanent resident alien? Temporary alien? Illegal alien? *Amnistía?* It mean I not American. I not vote, *nada*.

JUAN JOSÉ. *(cont.)* I am invisible. When first I come here, I prove I have the terrible danger in Mexico. So The Man he say I can be *Legal Alien.* Okay. But this is not enough for me man. I *need* it to be the U.S. Citizen. *Completamente.* My family in great danger.
I need this, man. I must do this. *Sí señor.* Then I bring my *Señora* here. My son also. To here…

SKINNY TIE 2. *(softly)* America.

JUAN JOSÉ. America. I was policeman there, yes, but I never take the bribe. *La mordida. Nunca. Los Narco-traficantes.* You know these bad guys?

SKINNY TIE 2. The cartel men who sell the drugs…

JUAN JOSÉ. Oh *sí.* Very-very bad guys. They are the most powerful. The most rich. They are the *Zetas,* man, they own the president and the governor and all the mayors. And they rent the people.

SKINNY TIE 1. Rent the people?

JUAN JOSÉ. Oh yes. This is for real. *Mira,* they can rent you to kill you *(pointing).* Then they rent the people to go to your *(pointing)* funeral and cry, they also rent a family to celebrate *your* life with very nice flowers. Then they rent the guy to go to prison for you who *kill* you. *La renta…*

SKINNY TIE 2. This is a *real* thing?

JUAN JOSÉ. It is a Mexican thing! But they will never own, never rent Juan José. Never. The drug war is very-very real man.

SKINNY TIE 1. *(offering softly and helpful)* We have Cupcake Wars here.

JUAN JOSÉ. I prefer your terrible wars. My war force me to leave my land, my señora Lydia-Esperanza and the baby boy.

SKINNY TIE 1. Esperanza means hope?

JUAN JOSÉ. Mexican hope. Not Obama Hope.

SKINNY TIE 2. And you've never seen your baby?

JUAN JOSÉ. No *señor,* he was born when I walk to here.

SKINNY TIE 2. You walked to America son?

JUAN JOSÉ. *(serious and fatigue)* But I sing most of the way. They will keep coming. And hiding in the shadows but for me, man I need most than anything in the world to pass this *pinche* US citizenship test *mañana.* I *must* do this important thing. For my family... I study so hard man, but now my God I so nervous, I forget *mucho.* I think I have Mexican ADD, and I stressed out man like I drink ten venti cappuccino with foams from Estarbucks or something... I no sleep in so many days...

SKINNY TIE 2. You've made amazing progress in the short time we've known you.

JUAN JOSÉ. The Catholic guy say the same thing to me but I quit him for Presbyterian guy – but he was so taciturn that I thought I kill him – and then I meet the Unitarian guy and he get naked for me so I run like *loco* out of his yurt and find the Scientology guy but I fail his personality test and so now I am here with you nice guys. *(brightly)* I choose you! See?

SKINNY TIE 1. Juan José, I want to follow up on something you said.

JUAN JOSÉ. *Claro que sí Brother Clark...*

SKINNY TIE 1. I understand you *need* to be an American...

JUAN JOSÉ. *Sí señor.* I need for sure this.

SKINNY TIE 1. But do you *want* to be an American?

SKINNY TIE 2. Have we lost leave of our manners Brother Clark?

SKINNY TIE 1. The differences between *need* and *want* is vast Elder Lew...

JUAN JOSÉ. It the same thing for me man: I *need* – I *want* – I *must!*

SKINNY TIE 1. But we're failing to see the...

SKINNY TIE 2. Okay. Okay. Enough. Enough. Semantics.

SKINNY TIE 1. I apologize...

JUAN JOSÉ. Do not apologize *Hermano* Clark, you are a good Spanish Inquisitor.

SKINNY TIE 2. *Bueno.* Let us move on, shall we?

JUAN JOSÉ. *Si porque* must study my Civic Flash Cards and my Citizen's Almanac very-very hard...

SKINNY TIE 2. I'll come here early in the morning, I'll baptize you myself and drive you to your exam. Okay *amigo?*

JUAN JOSÉ. I am grateful for this. You are my *new* friends for sure.

SKINNY TIE 1. That we are Juan Jose.

SKINNY TIE 2. And, we have a little gift for you.

> *(Lights shift rapidly. Two Mexican Police Officers enter wearing drab uniforms with bright yellow stripes down the outer pant leg.)*

> *(A low electronic throb pulsates: cheap Mexican electricity.)*

> *(**SKINNY TIE** 1 and 2 move into the upstage shadows.)*

> *(**CROOKED COP 2** places a Mexican cop hat on **JUAN JOSÉ**.)*

> *(**CROOKED COP 1** holds out a brown letter size envelope with a visible cartel stamp [Mexican skull]: cash)*

JUAN JOSÉ. You have gift for me?

CROOKED COP #1. *Un regalito, para ti cabrón... ¿Qué pasó Juan Jose? Es tuyo guey...*

CROOKED COP #2. Merry Chree-mass and a Happy New Jear...

> *(He tosses the tainted envelope on the table.)*

JUAN JOSÉ. But I did nothing to deserve this.

CROOKED COP #2. *Exacto.* And continue to do *nada* and there will be more.

> *(The **COPS** slowly circle **JUAN JOSÉ** like Mexican sharks.)*

CROOKED COP #1. You are a very good Mexican Policeman Juan José.

> *(CROOKED COP 1 is slyly checking for wires on JUAN JOSÉ's upper shoulders as he slowly crosses behind him.)*

Just like your grandfather. *¿Su abuelo eh compadre?*

JUAN JOSÉ. But if I accept this *regalo*, I will be in some sort of big trouble no? Something like this for sure...

CROOKED COP #2. We are poor. We take the money. We do not ask why.

JUAN JOSÉ. But we take The Oath.

CROOKED COP #1. We take The Mexican oath *cabrón*.

CROOKED COP #2. Take it Juan José. Think of your *familia*...

> *(An upstage door slides or swings open revealing – JUAN JOSÉ's pregnant wife – she looks down on the action from high.)*

LYDIA. Think of the things we can buy at the new Wal-Mart.

JUAN JOSÉ. Lydia. *Mi amor.* We have Wal-Mart in Sinaloa?

LYDIA. Three of them! And they are shiny and beautiful and they have the new GMO corns on the cobs and the baby will need many *cosas*. We *need* money husband!

JUAN JOSÉ. *(softly)* Lydia Esperanza!

> *(With a slight panic and surprised excitement of a contraction:)*

LYDIA. Husband!

> *(LYDIA is gone. JUAN JOSÉ slowly lifts up the dirty envelope.)*

JUAN JOSÉ. If I take this, what I have to do? Something for *sure?*

CROOKED COP #2. *Nada cabrón. Nada!* And continue to do nothing.

> *(JUAN JOSÉ lays the jack back on the table.)*

> *(CROOKED COP explodes off his chair charging at JJ.)*

CROOKED COP #1. *You refuse our gift cabrón? Te crees que estás más mejor que nosotros cabrón? Te mato cabrón. ¡Te mato! [threat on his life]*

JUAN JOSÉ. *Claro que NO Luis Andres...*

> (**JUAN JOSÉ** *stands ready to defend like a learned boxer.*)

> (**CROOKED COP 2** *settles his partner down then works on* **JJ**.)

CROOKED COP #2. *Cálmate, cálmate! (Good Cop Bad Cop in any language).* They will come for you. The *Carteles*. And they will rent him to visit your *familia...*

CROOKED COP #1. And then they will rent me to express my outrage and sympathy to the press. But only a little bit *pescadito. ¿Sabes?*

CROOKED COP #2. We are rent-a-cops.

CROOKED COP #1. Sit here then with your God's and your fucking principles and think about what you are doing *pinche fresa... (with a quick and expert snort of meth off his upper palm)*

> (**COP 1** *is amped and dripping in the back of his throat.*)

> (**JUAN JOSÉ** *slowly takes re-possession of the envelope.*)

CROOKED COP #2. *(chummy) A sí me gusto!* I knew you would not disappoint us. Good Mexican.

CROOKED COP # 1. *(chummy too)* Good Mexican!

> (**CROOKED COP 1** *removes* **JJ**'s *cop hat and kisses the top of his head like an uncle. With a sudden bright idea to his partner.*)

Hey, let's go to the new Olive Garden *cabrón!*

> *(Bad* **COPS** *exit.)*

> (**JUAN JOSÉ** *waits for* **COPS** *exit then rips the envelope in two.*)

(Lights restore. **SKINNY TIES** *move back down from shadows:)*

SKINNY TIE 2. Take the gift Juan José.

*(***SKINNY TIE*** *still holding out the wrapped gift:)*

JUAN JOSÉ. If I accept this gift, what I have to do?

SKINNY TIE 1. *Nada, amigo, nada.*

SKINNY TIE 2. May it comfort you on your long night of study.

(He rips into it and must mask his disappointment at:)

JUAN JOSÉ. Oh thank you. The Church of Jesus Christ of Latter Day Saints. *Qué lindo...* It smell so fresh and nice. Oh I very much like the new American books.

SKINNY TIE 1. You *know* this book Juan José?

JUAN JOSÉ. I see The Mormon's book once before in Mexico but I not read it yet.

SKINNY TIE 2. No time like the present.

JUAN JOSÉ. *Claro que sí.* Hey could you guys get for me one comp ticket for *The Book of Mormon* show? Those guys they are LSD, right?

SKINNY TIE 1. LDS yes. And they're not comping.

SKINNY TIE 2. I should tell you son that stagecraft and non-profit theater is the devil's playground.

SKINNY TIE 1. We can only get you a ticket to meet our Lord The Sheppard.

JUAN JOSÉ. *(quiet awe)* The Chepper?

SKINNY TIE 2. Yes. For he awaits to bathe you in the blood of lambs.

JUAN JOSÉ. And *this* is better than non-profit theater?

SKINNY TIE 2. Why sweet gentle Jesus yes.

JUAN JOSÉ. *(polite)* Bummer mang. What else you got?

SKINNY TIE 2. Possible space-travel in the after life?

JUAN JOSÉ. El Star-chip Enterprise?

SKINNY TIE 1. Where no Mexican has gone before...

SKINNY TIE 2. Shall we pray in fellowship?

SKINNY TIE 1. What is it, *qué pasa Juan José?*

JUAN JOSÉ. Do I surrender to your God or to *mine?*

SKINNY TIE 1. Which God would you prefer?

JUAN JOSÉ. *(quite serious)* Whichever God help me be American faster.

SKINNY TIE 2. Our God will do.

> **(SKINNY TIES** *try to join hands* **JJ** *as he politely recoils.)*

JUAN JOSÉ. Maybe better we do this *mañana?*

SKINNY TIE 1. Are you sure?

JUAN JOSÉ. I think so, it is very late and I must *estudy* my book.

SKINNY TIE 2. For soon you shall be an American Citizen.

JUAN JOSÉ. *Americano...* This is my dream. *Mi sueño...* Hey do you guys know where I can sign up for the carpal tunnel syndrome?

SKINNY TIE 2. Are you hurt boy?

JUAN JOSÉ. No, no. I just wanted to feel like American. We are not allowed to have carpal tunnel in Mexico.

> **(SKINNY TIES** *are confused.)*

Man I can never repay you guys...

SKINNY TIE 2. Be it known unto all nations, kindreds, tongues, and people, that we shall sit in the Kingdom...

SKINNY TIE 1. For one day soon perhaps you can help us spread the Good News about religious circumcision in your Spanish tongue.

SKINNY TIE 2. Your journey, your trek, is not unlike that of our ancestors.

SKINNY TIE 1. Our Mormon Trail was bloody as yours.

SKINNY TIE 2. *Without* the drugs!

JUAN JOSÉ. I carry no *contraband...*

SKINNY TIE 2. You are a member of our Dark Tribe Juan José.

SKINNY TIE 1. The Lamanites!

JUAN JOSÉ. Lamanites?

SKINNY TIE 2. Old as the Land and the Land old as Oil.

> (*JUAN JOSÉ is confused then:*)

See, our people knew of inhospitable lands, great migrations. Our bloody trail *West*.

SKINNY TIE 1. You are walking to Zion JJ. *El Norte*. To your citizenship.

SKINNY TIE 2. To your New Jerusalem.

JUAN JOSÉ. Exodus...

SKINNY TIE 2. Exodus 22:21 – "Thou shalt neither vex nor oppress a stranger: for ye were strangers in the land of Egypt".

JUAN JOSÉ. *Hejole...* Mexicans in Egypt?!

SKINNY TIE 1. Hispanic's are the fastest growing members of our church.

JUAN JOSÉ. I know I was a size thirty when I leave Mexico.

SKINNY TIE 2. *Nuestra gente camina mucho en la noche también...*

> (*JUAN JOSÉ is impressed with the Spanish command.*)

Bueno, this man has much on his mind. Let us allow him rest.

JUAN JOSÉ. No-no sleepy tonight *señor*. I will study all the night!

SKINNY TIE 1. I did that in college, drink a Coke super fast!

SKINNY TIE 2. *(darkly grave)* There shall be no drinking of Coca Cola here tonight.

JUAN JOSÉ. *Espera un momentito*, I do have a question. *Si permites... Okay*, if America, she want to build a big wall to keep out the Mexicans, who do they think will build the wall?

> (**SKINNY TIES** *consider the question.*)

JUAN JOSÉ. The Mexicans will! And it will be a very professional wall, very beautiful. Sí. But we will know where the holes are so we can sneak back in.

SKINNY TIE 1. Oh snap! Ha ha ha… *(getting it and laughing crazy)*

> *(**SKINNY TIE 1** laughs but not.* **SKINNY TIE 2***)*

SKINNY TIE 2. Go wait in the car Rodney.

SKINNY TIE 1. Yes Elder Clark.

SKINNY TIE 2. And flog thyself but good son…

SKINNY TIE 1. *(quiet and sincere)* In obedience and perfect submission…

> *(**SKINNY TIE 1** slowly backs away into the shadows.)*

JUAN JOSÉ. "Book of Mormon: in case of emergency this book can be used as a floatation device. L.O.L Rodney…"

> *(**SKINNY TIE 2** slow burns to **SKINNY TIE 1**, he darts off stage.)*

SKINNY TIE 2. *Hasta mañana Juan José.*

> *(Then with seriousness and a caring hand touching* **JJ** *'s heart:)*

Study our sacred history books with fervor, son.

JUAN JOSÉ. Yessir. *Claro que sí* Elder Lewis.

> *(Elder exits.* **JUAN JOSÉ** *opens the Mormon Book. He smells it newness, its American-ness. It comforts him somehow.)*

*Libros, libros…*too many books!

> *(He closes the LDS book and opens his Citizen's Almanac.)*

No sleepy-sleep Juan José.

> *(He turns on a small battery powered radio at low level.)*

(Radio dial settles a Billie Holliday song about "Dreams" –)

JUAN JOSÉ. *(reading)* "We hold these Truths to be self-evident, that all Men are created equal, that they are endowed by their Creator with certain unalienable Rights, that among these are Life, Liberty and the pursuit of Happiness." Wow. What beautiful promise they make to me… I want to exist here. Just do it *loco*…

(He yawns exhaustion setting in.)

Flash cards, flash cards! Okay *bueno*…

(JUAN JOSÉ lightly slaps his face to keep alert.)

When do we celebrate Independence Day? *Cinco de Mayo! No manches.* The Fourth of July. Man, I am going to esmoke this test! Next *carta!* Name the original Thirteen Colonies. Thirteen Colonies sound like a gang. *Chingow* this test is going to be hard.

(Another Flash Card even later in the night: Time lapse –)

Next: Why do Chicanos love Morrissey? *(quietly sings)* I AM HUMAN AND I NEED TO BE LOVED.
It is a conundrum. Be serious Juan Jose! Okay…

(He changes the radio to help concentration as it skips over a dodger game and lands on a song he likes – the band america on easy listening station singing mid-song "Ventura Highway."*)

(JJ somehow knows the chorus and sounds funny singing…)

ALLIGATOR LIZARDS IN THE AIR… IN THE AIR…

Back to the test! Name one war fought by the US in the 1800s? I know this: The Mexican American War. *Hejole* I am getting sleepy Mexican Syndrome from too much reading. I will succumb to my slumbers!

---

* Please see Music Use Note on page 3

(The weight of **JJ** *'s sleepy Mexican head is slowly pulling him down to the table – in the instant* **JJ** *'s head hits the table after long cartoon snore:)*

(Huge gun and cannon blasts!)

(The physical world around him changes in an instant:)

(We are suddenly at the altar of old Cathedral of Guadalupe at La Villa Hidalgo just north of Mexico City.)

(Box car and border walls open to reveal The Black Saint – St. Adrian of Nicomedia – Patron Saint of Arms Dealers and Narcos standing high near the Stained Glass and surrounded by flickering red candles.)

(Gun blasts and cannon fire punctuate the urgent proceedings.)

(Enter US Representative **NICHOLAS TRIST**, *a US Cavalry Troop and an American Attaché in bowler hat as well as the Mexican Officers and Government Man Luis and Bernardo.)*

(All create a sort of antique painting then:)

(A huge cannon blast pushes the "painting" into action.)

NICHOLAS TRIST. *Señores!* President Polk is not a patient man.

(The Mexicans confer and grumble.)

Your signature Juan José!

JUAN JOSÉ. What am I signing?

COUTO. *(grim)* The Treaty of Guadalupe Hidalgo.

*(***CUOTO*** double checks the document on podium in horror.)*

CUEVAS. *(matter of fact translation)* El Tratado de Guadalupe Hidalgo.

JUAN JOSÉ. Oh my God... Really?

> (*A* **LARGE MEXICAN WOMAN** *with a sash bearing the colors of the Mexican standard quietly weeps and works with an cordless floor buffer with text: Property of Mexico. Shelling abound:*)

NICHOLAS TRIST. Mexico City is under complete US occupation as we speak. And her retreat is only possible after you cede parts of Colorado, Arizona, New Mexico and the Wyoming territories to the US government.

JUAN JOSÉ. He is *keeding* right?

> (**CUOTO** *gravely shakes his head "no" from the dais.*)

NICHOLAS TRIST. In addition we shall receive the California and Nevada Territories.

CUEVAS. It is a cold dark day in the Land of the Serpent and Eagle!

> (*Huge blast sending* **JUAN JOSÉ** *to the church floor.*)

JUAN JOSÉ. *Híjole* what does Mexico get?

NICHOLAS TRIST. We guarantee that all Mexican citizens currently living in the Territories will receive American Citizenship.

JUAN JOSÉ. Son of a *beech* I missed *that* boat!

NICHOLAS TRIST. We shall like to annex Texas, Utah and parts of Oregon.

COUTO. Oregon no! I give you South El Monte adjacent to gentrify like you did Williamsburg but not Oregon!

NICHOLAS TRIST. Oregon *sí!*

LARGE MEXICAN WOMAN. *(mournful moan)* ¡Ay, mi Lindo México!

NICHOLAS TRIST. Weep not large Mexican gentlewoman, for I will care for you as a father does for an illegitimate child. Now go fetch papa a spittoon...

> (*With a hard slap on her generous Mexican bottom.*)

LARGE MEXICAN WOMAN. *Aye, bruto. (breathy if not a touch sexy)*

NICHOLAS TRIST. Okey-Dokey. Who will sign my Treaty?

JUAN JOSÉ. How many people die in this Mexican-American War?

NICHOLAS TRIST. Tens of thousands!

CUEVAS. Surely more…

JUAN JOSÉ. And my signature will end the bloodshed?

> *(***CUOTO** *pulls* **JUAN JOSÉ** *down stage for an urgent word.)*

COUTO. My beloved Moore may I speak to you in *semi-privado-soto* voice? Your signature makes an outlaw of any Mexican ever wishing to enter the United States. Ever!

JUAN JOSÉ. Ever?

COUTO. *Sí!* Your signature, without question give away 1/18 of the entire continent forever shifting the tectonic narrative of the Americas my Lord!

CUEVAS. He must sign! The killing must stop.

JUAN JOSÉ. Killing? No! I only want to be American.

> *(***JJ** *moves toward the podium.)*

COUTO. But you are Mexican!

> *(***CUEVAS** *and* **CUOTO** *struggle over* **JJ** *with the feathered pen.)*

CUEVAS. His signature ends the bloodshed! .

COUTO. Let the bloodshed continue!

> *(***CUOTO** *yanks the Feathered Pen lodging in heart.)*

Son of a bitch that fancy fathered pen smarts!

> *(He turns to all with great drama and flair:)*

The *San Patricios* have joined us in *Churrabasco* with great dispatch. Surely a conscripted Irish farmer knows how to lay a Yankee in his grave…

(A smile and dig for **TRYSTE** *who volleys with a tip of hat.)*

JUAN JOSÉ. I hate to be the one to tell you this, but Mexico will never ever defeat the Americans...

(JJ walks over and pulls the Feathered Pen from **CUOTO***'s chest.)*

COUTO. *¡Ay Dios!* *(reacting to pen removal)*

*(***COUTO*** cocks a revolver and moves in at* **JUAN JOSÉ***'s head.)*

Do not sign that document Juan José.

(A low pulsating sound throbs.)

CUEVAS. Sign the document now peasant!

*(***CUEVAS*** now points his revolver at* **JUAN JOSÉ***'s head.)*

NICHOLAS TRIST. *Híjole,* such a passionate and folkloric people!

JUAN JOSÉ. I don't know what to do...

NICHOLAS TRIST. *(Victorian evangelical fervor)* The die has been cast!

JUAN JOSÉ. Alas. I should sign, but... *(confused stall)*

NICHOLAS TRIST. What part of surrender does the simple Mexican *not* understand?

JUAN JOSÉ/CUOTO/CUEVAS. *Simple...?*

COUTO. Hath not a Mexican eyes?

(With great Shakespearian simmer and flourish:)

Hath not a Mexican hands, organs, dimensions, senses, affect ions, passions; fed with the same food, hurt by the same weapon, suffer the same disease as the Gringo? If you prick us, do we not bleed man? If you tickle our *testículos,* do we not laugh? If you wrong us shall we not avenge, *cabrón Treest*?! *(Tryst)*

*(***CUOTO*** points revolver to* **TRIST** *then at his own chest. Bam!)*

COUTO. Aye there is *blood! Blood! Blood! Blood! Blood!*

> *(Pulling crimson fabric/entrails from inside his vest.)*

> *(Holding for a final dramatic flourish:)*

Manifest Destiny hath robbed us of our *Tierra y Libertad! Grathias. (with Victorian bow)*

ST. ADRIAN. Drama queen...

COUTO. Hey...

> *(JUAN JOSÉ holds the feathered pen high above his head:)*

JUAN JOSÉ. I cannot stop history. I will sign...

> *(Time slows.)*

> *(The Feathered Pen is slowly lowered to the podium as it nears the signing of the Treaty.)*

> *(The instant pen touches parchment paper the world swirls ever fast:)*

> *(Quickly enter Two MODERN BORDER PATROL OFFICERS.)*

> *(Hear: "Bad Boys Bad Boys (What you gonna do?)"* Deafening Helicopters.)*

TOUGH FEMALE BORDER OFFICER. Okay everybody hands in the air! Identification now.

> *(Only JUAN JOSÉ and CUEVAS remain. They comply.)*

JUAN JOSÉ. I have no identification... I have only US flashcards!

TOUGH FEMALE BORDER OFFICER. Oh no she di'int gurl...

TOUGH MALE BORDER OFFICER. Keep those hands where I can see them*!*

JUAN JOSÉ. *Jessir!*

---

* Please see Music Use Note on page 3

TOUGH FEMALE BORDER OFFICER. *(in radio)* Smokey-smokey, I have two suspected illegal aliens in Secondary Inspection over!

TOUGH MALE BORDER OFFICER. Which one of you Hispanic geniuses just signed the Treaty of Guadalupe?

> (**CUEVAS** *and* **JUAN JOSÉ** *pointing at each other.*)

CUEVAS.	**JUAN JOSÉ.**
He did.	She did.

TOUGH MALE BORDER OFFICER. That makes you Illegal Aliens effective immediately. On your knees!

TOUGH FEMALE BORDER OFFICER. Spread those legs player-player...

> (*expertly and swiftly kicking the limbs out*)

JUAN JOSÉ. May I please have a moment with my wife?

TOUGH MALE BORDER OFFICER. Whad'ya you got in the bag? Drugs? Out of state fruit? Don't lie to me now, son...

JUAN JOSÉ. Lydia-Esperanza say something!

CUEVAS. *¡Cállate cabrón!*

TOUGH FEMALE BORDER OFFICER. Aha! *(found)* A feathered pen!

> (**JJ** *reaches for pen out of instinct.*)

TOUGH MALE BORDER OFFICER. I said stay down!

> (*Hitting* **JUAN JOSÉ** *with baton.*)

> (**FEMALE OFFICER** *on shoulder radio:*)

TOUGH FEMALE BORDER OFFICER. I have two highly agitated Hispanic males requesting back up, over!

> (**MALE BORDER COP** *finds a suspicious books Holding one up.*)

TOUGH MALE BORDER OFFICER. What the hell is this?

JUAN JOSÉ. *That* is the Book from the Mormons guys...

TOUGH MALE BORDER OFFICER. The Koran! Holy camel shit!

JUAN JOSÉ. *Por favor* Lydia-Esperanza you *must* talk to me *mi amor...*

CUEVAS. I am not Lydia!

> *(BORDER OFFICER removes CUEVAS' hat. Her hair falls!)*

CUEVAS/LYDIA. You got me. I am Lydia.

> *(LYDIA calmly unpeels her mustache off.)*

TOUGH FEMALE BORDER OFFICER. This here some sick-ass Tranny mess. Over.

TOUGH MALE BORDER OFFICER. Back-to-back detainees! Back to back now! Sergeant, I think I got me a terrorist over here.

> *(The Detainees are B-2-B as the COPS confer in that cop way.)*

JUAN JOSÉ. *Mi amor* I knew it! Why are you here?

CUEVAS/LYDIA. You are always in trouble. Everybody is mad at you.

JUAN JOSÉ. Why are you nagging me, wife?

CUEVAS/LYDIA. I am not nagging you! I am *saving* you. What happened to you?

> *(CUEVAS/LYDIA reaches for JUAN JOSÉ's face.)*

TOUGH MALE BORDER OFFICER. *No toco! No toco!*

TOUGH FEMALE BORDER OFFICER. Smokey-smokey I have a domestic dispute in progress.

BARELY INTELLIGIBLE PATROL RADIO. Delta-Tango-Bravo-Zulu-Spear-chucker-churros. Over!

TOUGH MALE BORDER OFFICER. Copy!

TOUGH FEMALE BORDER OFFICER. Clear!

TOUGH MALE BORDER OFFICER. We will be back to tazer gun you both in the buttock area.

TOUGH FEMALE BORDER OFFICER. *(Holding up the feathered pen)* Contrabando!

> *(BORDER PATROL OFFICERS exit on line:)*

Where the damn donut shop? I need me a got damn churro!

(*JUAN JOSÉ is drawn close to* CUEVAS *' neck locket.*)

CUEVAS/LYDIA. He look just like you, *papi.*

JUAN JOSÉ. *Mi hijo lindo, mi Juan Josécito...*

(*They kiss gentle. Automatic gunfire erupts off stage.*)

CARTEL GOON. (*offstage*) *Juan Jose! ¡Estoy buscándote cabrón!*

(*The married couple leap to their feet quick like.*)

CUEVAS/LYDIA. The *Cartel* is here! You must run now Juan José. Run!

JUAN JOSÉ. I will protect you and the baby...

CUEVAS/LYDIA. My God the baby! Come on Juan José, run, run!

JUAN JOSÉ. *I can't!*

(**LYDIA** *is slowly lowered slowly down the center trap door.*)

(*JUAN JOSÉ's legs are frozen like a bad dream −*)

CUEVAS/LYDIA. I am melting! I am melting. Very slowly... *Adios amor...*

JUAN JOSÉ. Until next time *mon amor!*

CUEVAS/LYDIA. *Until next time...*

(*The stage rapidly shifts to yet another place: Juarez Factory.*)

(*Narco banda music and factory sounds as we hear the radio:*)

NPR AUDIO VOICE. *The human face of NAFTA can be seen in the violent border towns like Juarez and Tijuana, it is the face of the poor. As American productivity shifts to these shantytowns local drug cartels are pressed into service as the de-facto security arm of the US Maquiladoras. The Dow Index rose sharply today with news of large profits for the makers of genetically modified corn and in other news...*

(*Mexican factory workers push carts and prepare.*)

(**JUAN JOSÉ** *finds himself in a Nike shoe factory.*)

(*He turns a large factory wheel activating the conveyer belt.*)

(*Shoe-boxes bearing the unmistakable Nike logo and green and gold of the Oregon Ducks move down the belt.*)

(*Buzzers buzz. Bells ring: Lunchtime!*)

(*The First Worker [*CARTEL GOON 1*] leads* **JUAN JOSÉ** *downstage.*)

(*He opens his lunch box and offers bags of white powder and huge cash roll to a scared and back stepping* **JUAN JOSÉ.***)

(*The worker whips out a pistol from his lunch box.*)

(*Another* **CARTEL GOON 2** *in cowboy hat enters with an UZI.*)

(*Narco banda music makes for a grotesque Mexican Vaudeville as* **GOONS** *spray bullets with* **JUAN JOSÉ** *stick in the crossfire:*)

(**JUAN JOSÉ** *dies 1000 cartoon deaths in hail of bullets.*)

(*Gun fire and music stops abruptly.*)

DRUG CARTEL GOON 1. *¡Hasta mañana, amigo!*

DRUG CARTEL GOON 2. This must be what they call a cycle of violence!

(**GOONS** *exit laughing. NPR Tag:*)

NPR AUDIO VOICE. *Juan José the US Citizen hopeful is still dreaming and amazingly studying his US Flashcard, a sign of his unyielding determination to be American perhaps…*

(**JUAN JOSÉ** *is prone on a rock that has been set.*)

(*He slowly reaches to make sure all his parts are in-tact, relieved he pops up and continues with his US flashcards.*)

JUAN JOSÉ. My determination, *sí! Bueno,* name an American Indian Tribe in the United States? Okay. Cherokee. What territory did the United States buy from the Frenchies in 1803? The Louisiana Purchase *creo...*

> *(Factory is completely gone – a deer appears on a Soda Machine.)*

> *(Snow falls as* **TWO AMERICAN EXPLORERS** *enter in a wooden canoe.)*

EXPLORER 1. Meriwether, I've just discovered a man on a rock!

EXPLORER 2. A lost Mexican Gold Miner perhaps?

EXPLORER 1. A wayward Spanish Fur Trapper? What shall we name it?

EXPLORER 2. I shall call him Trader Joe.

EXPLORER 1. What is that flat thing you eat?

JUAN JOSÉ. My last organic corn tortilla.

> *(They climb out of the wooden canoe.)*

EXPLORER 2. How ever does it work?

JUAN JOSÉ. Put the Soyrizo-beaver-meat inside and make burrito!

EXPLORER 2. I shall call it a wrap.

EXPLORER 1. Your provisions are lifting our spirits. We thank you.

JUAN JOSÉ. *No hay de que...*

EXPLORER 1. I am Mister Clark, this exquisite half-starved and medicated white man is Meriwether Lewis!

JUAN JOSÉ. *Hijo* man I meet the great Clark and Jerry Lewis?!

LEWIS. The Great Lewis, *then* Clark...

CLARK. Hark...

JUAN JOSÉ. Hark...

> *(Enter: Buckskins and plastic trinkets. A baby in a papoose is on her back.)*

(An external metallic Dental Guard around her mouth remind us that Sacagawea is young. She sprays a bit when she speaks.)

SACAGAWEA. Fur Trappers ahead, trading diseased pelts. We avoid them or shoot them on sight.

JUAN JOSÉ. My God. *La Saca-Chihuahua.* The great Indian Woman on my US dollar coin!

LEWIS. Mother *fucker* minted before us! We suck…

JUAN JOSÉ. *La Saca-chihuahua…* How cool is this?

SACAGAWEA. Who is this strange man who butchers my name?

JUAN JOSÉ. I am the great Juan José?

(Unsure but with the Victorian bow he learned from CUOTO.)

SACAGAWEA. You must leave my camp immediately.

LEWIS. *Por qué* why?

SACAGAWEA. He likely carries small pox or measles or Mexican mono.

CLARK. Oh my.

*(**CLARK** quickly hand sanitize with small bottle.)*

LEWIS. Best leave him for bear!

JUAN JOSÉ. El Poo Bear *que curioso…* Man, this is too many, *(much)* I estudy you in my book la Sac-Chihuahua. You lead these famous men even though you are only fifteen years old.

SACAGAWEA. Fifteen and a half!

JUAN JOSÉ. *Perdon.* Your beautiful name Saca-chihuahua mean many things…

LEWIS. Like Boat Launcher…

CLARK. Or Leads The Young Nation on Sacred Golden Stripper Pole.

JUAN JOSÉ. *OR,* Mother of Beautiful Baby Boy!

SACAGAWEA. Silence! *(dental guard spit)*

CLARK. What is it mother/child?

SACAGAWEA. Beaverhead Gorge is near. We are close to Three Forks. I have put Lewis and Clark back on the proper trail.

LEWIS. Another excellent job, American guys.

CLARK. We're out. Westward whores!

JUAN JOSÉ. I mean no disrespect but according to my J U. S. History book...

CLARK. The History of the Jews...? *(a grim pronouncement)*

JUAN JOSÉ. Not that Good Book. No. My special *libro, aquí. Mira...*

> *(**JUAN JOSÉ** opens his book and a page unfolds 20 feet.)*
>
> *(Magic sounds and lights focus on the long "corridor of pages" which reveal a huge and helpful map never before seen.)*
>
> *(**SACA** is pulled down to the map. L and C hover about in awe. **JUAN JOSÉ** pushes sensing an in or friendship with **SACA**.)*

Many miles ahead, you will find the Snake River, it will swallow you but the Columbia River is passable...

LEWIS. But only here...

SACAGAWEA. I totally knew that! *(defensive)*

JUAN JOSÉ. Many days from now you will come to a big fork: The South Fork is the Donner Party trail: *(beat) Do not go this way.*

CLARK. My God man! Look at the clarity of these illustrations...

LEWIS. Topography, scale even rainfall!

JUAN JOSÉ. You see?

LEWIS. Look, Meriwether Lewis State Park. How bitch'n is that?

CLARK. Clark National Forrest. Ha!

LEWIS. I want a forest...

JUAN JOSÉ. You have a rock outcropping *there...*

(**CLARK** *pulls* **LEWIS** *downstage a few feet.*)

CLARK. *(concern)* Meriwether, nothing to honor Sacagawea?

LEWIS. Oh sure, look: Squaw Valley, Mohegan Sun, Morongo Casino!

SACAGAWEA. What's this big Blue Snake with a number on it?

JUAN JOSÉ. That is the I-5 Corridor.

CLARK. Thank you Juan José. You are welcome to join our expedition anytime...

JUAN JOSÉ. *No gracias señor*, I must respect Sacagawea's *espace...*

LEWIS. May your families multiply and prosper in our Blue State territories...

CLARK. And may your country send ours more left handed pitchers as we welcome you with open arms and a loaded shotgun with safety lock on!

LEWIS. God speed then young sire. Moving out!
Lively now!

(**LEWIS** *and* **CLARK** *climb back into the wooden canoe and exit as:*)

CLARK. *(singing like Crosby and Hope)*
"OH WE'RE OFF ON THE ROAD TO MOROCCO..."

LEWIS. Take the Siskiyou Pass the freeway is backed up... Four!

(*They move off as something crashes back stage:*)

SACAGAWEA. You think you are *so* smart Spanish...

JUAN JOSÉ. I was impressive for a Mexican no?

(*He magically removes the coin from behind her ear.*)

(*She studies her image on it.*)

SACAGAWEA. *(studying the coin)* I look fat... (*sounding as any American teen*)

JUAN JOSÉ. No, no...

SACAGAWEA. You're cute, *and* arrogant like my French husband...

JUAN JOSÉ. You are strong like my Mexican wife.

SACAGAWEA. Where is she?

JUAN JOSÉ. In Mexico taking care of our son...

> (**SACAGAWEA** *signs silent for:*)

SACAGAWEA. (*US sign language*) Do you miss them?

> (**JUAN JOSÉ** *understands:*)

JUAN JOSÉ. Oh yes, I miss them very much. So much my heart is bleeding.

> (*touching his heart*)

SACAGAWEA. My feet are bleeding.

JUAN JOSÉ. I can help you...

> (*Old Factory whistle blows:*)

> (*Center doors slide open revealing a* **GRIZZLY BEAR** *with 3 Nike Shoe Boxes from the Juarez Factory –* **JUAN JOSÉ** *fetches.*)

JUAN JOSÉ. Thank you Grizzly Bear!

KYLE THE FACTORY BEAR. Go Bruins!

> (*Mister Bear masturbates like a just woke bear as doors close.*)

JUAN JOSÉ. Here take these.

SACAGAWEA. What is it?

JUAN JOSÉ. NIKE. Waterproof. Oregon Duck sneakers. You will need these for The Trail. Take a pair for Señor Lewis and one for Sr. Clark.

SACAGAWEA. *Cool!* I shall run like the Puma.

JUAN JOSÉ. Just Do It, *loca!*

> (*The multi-cultural Trail Cook* **HOP LING** *arrives dragging a contained campfire by a rope to down center near the rock.*)

SACAGAWEA. Here comes Hop Ling, put-upon trail cook for lost White Man.

HOP LING. Who are *you?*

JUAN JOSÉ. I am Juan José Lost Mexican.

HOP LING. I give to you most benevolent friend: free-range jack-rabbit from Whole Foods. Organic, *and* kosher.

JUAN JOSÉ. Kosher? *Gracias* Hip Hop Ling. Excuse me but you are African and Jewish *and* Chino?

HOP LING. I am American. What is Juan José?

JUAN JOSÉ. I am in between countries right now. But *mañana* I be something for sure I hope!

HOP LING. Keep hope alive man. Believe you can Bro and you are halfway there…

JUAN JOSÉ. Tony and Maria say this in *West Side Story?*

HOP LING. No sir. Teddy Roosevelt!

JUAN JOSÉ. Ah, *gracias* Hip Hop Ling.

HOP LING. *De nada* player… *De nada*… Shalom!

>   (**SACAGAWEA** *fist bumps* **HIP HOP LING**.)

>   (*He exits with nike boxes singing his Mitzvah Song.*)

JUAN JOSÉ. How cool is it that we find each other on the Pacific Crest Trail?

SACAGAWEA. I am on The Trail. You are in a Spirit Dream.

JUAN JOSÉ. I hope your people will be kind to you…

SACAGAWEA. Why wouldn't they be?

>   (*There is only silence as* **JUAN JOSÉ** *struggles for words.*)

> (*almost hurt*) Why wouldn't they be?

>   (*Lights soften as the day slowly takes flight into night.*)

JUAN JOSÉ. Some might say you are like a sell-out, a traitor, who only facilitate the onslaught. Like *la Malinche* with Cortéz…

SACAGAWEA. And what will you say Juan José?

(Lovely-lovely guitar as lights soften gently.)

JUAN JOSÉ. I would say that your youthful laughter around the campfire with your little son must have meant so much to these brave and lonely men.

(A Bird softly chirps its "binding song" in the high canopy.)

SACAGAWEA. *(sounding of a woman)* Look, a double-crested blue jay.

(The Blue Jay is a hopeful omen.)

JUAN JOSÉ. *(eyes closing)* You are a dream *inside* a dream...

(Slowly lowers her dental guard and not sounding like **LYDIA**.*)*

SACAGAWEA. Come back home to me Juan José... Come home...

(SACAGAWEA *becoming a woman before our eyes and is now gone.)*

JUAN JOSÉ. Lydia!!!

KYLE THE FACTORY BEAR. Rooooaaarrr!!!

(The **GRIZZLY BEAR** *has entered.)*

(Shotgun blast! The **BEAR** *is hit.)*

TEDDY ROOSEVELT. Right between his hairy balls!

(KYLE *turns and whips off his bear head to expose the actor.)*

KYLE THE BEAR. Oh son of a bitch! *Right* in the lower Rush Limbaugh's... I'll never need contraception from the government again. Fuck me!

(KYLE *sounds like a wounded ChewBacca from Star Wars as he limps off.* **TEDDY** *moves in on* **JUAN JOSÉ** *and the space.)*

TEDDY ROOSEVELT. I like your dash kid. Take a knee, look here, Keep your eyes on the Stars, and your Feet on the Ground!

JUAN JOSÉ. Okay *Señor Presidente.*

TEDDY ROOSEVELT. Call me Teddy, excuse me...

> *(He aims and fires. Shotgun blast.)*

Ah, bully-bully... Almost got him! There is not a man among us who does not at times need a helping hand to be out to him, and shame upon him who will not stretch out the helping hand to his brother, excuse me!

> *(Another shotgun blast, a car crashes violently.)*

Stop texting! Damn Subaru drivers. Remember Juan José: just because you have a pretty little mouth don't mean you were born to suck!

JUAN JOSÉ. This is estrange thing for a president to say, no?

TEDDY ROOSEVELT. Bubba Clinton who? Well then, speak softly *in English* and carry a Big Shtick!

JUAN JOSÉ. Okay Teddy!

> *(Another shot from **TEDDY**. Large Elephant roar is heard.)*

TEDDY ROOSEVELT. Bully! Killed the GOP Elephant. *You're welcome!*

> (**TEDDY** *is gone.*)

> *(Transition to West Texas 1918:)*

> *(A wooden Grave Marker is placed on the edge of the stage. The Campfire and Rock are there from before. As we hear:)*

RADIO VOICE. *The H1N1 form swine flu virus is a close descendant of the Spanish influenza that caused an estimated fifty million deaths in 1918...*

> *(Sorrowful and soulful guitar of *Lead Belly swirls.)*

> *(Lead Belly was chased by Texas Law Men during this time.)*

> *(A Tumbleweed moves across upstage.)*

(The shadow of a huge lone Mesquite Tree provides a moving gobo on a white US Army Tent that rises from the floor.)

(The tent should have an amber light source from within which provides scarce hearth for these lonely plains.)

(We are one hundred yards west of the Marathon Cemetery: The actual place where **VIOLA** *pitched her "US Army Flu tent."* **JUAN JOSÉ** *is pulled low to a crude wooden grave marker:)*

JUAN JOSÉ. *(reads marker)* Novella Pettus… Born 1903. Depart this world September five, 1918. Beloved daughter of Ben and Viola Pettus. Marathon *Texas?* What in the heck is going on now, 1918?

(Big gun click.)

(A man resplendent in full Ku Klux Klan garb enters with a loaded German Luger pointed at the back of **JJ**'s *head.)*

MAN IN ROBE. Stand up Mexican!

*(***JUAN JOSÉ*** slowly rises and turns toward the voice.)*

What'chu doing on this side of the Border, boy?

JUAN JOSÉ. Dreaming?

MAN IN ROBE. Thought I run all you wetbacks 'cross the river last Night?

JUAN JOSÉ. I was with Saca-chihuahua and the South Park guys last night.

MAN IN ROBE. Prepare to meet your Maker boy.

*(***MAN*** pulls back the cocking slide of the lugar.)*

*(***VIOLA PETTUS***: self-taught African-American Nurse emerges from her tent with her loaded shotgun pointed at KKK Man.)*

VIOLA. What be your business in my camp mister?

(KKK Man hesitates — **VIOLA** *pumps her shotgun.)*

MAN IN ROBE. My baby! The baby...she's in a terrible way... I need your help Viola Pettus.

> *(***BEN PETTUS,*** *Black Cowboy — weary and wise — enter from tent.)*

VIOLA. Where the child be now Klansman?

MAN IN ROBE. Yonder automobile. She won't make it to Ft. Stockton. Help us!

VIOLA. I cannot help you with that *pistola* pointed at the boy's head. Kindly holster your iron before I put a cap in *your* head. Sir.

> *(***MAN IN ROBE*** *lowers his iron shaky.)*

Now take them sheets from around your head. I be need'n 'em inside my tent.

> *(Infant cries in the distance. KKK Man removes his robe revealing hard shoes and sox held up by garters — no pants.)*

Time *be* wasting now!

> *(The* **ROBED MAN** *shuffles and slowly removes his head sheet.)*

Judge? *(not totally surprised)*

MAN IN ROBE. Miss Viola. How do Ben...?

BEN. Your Honor...

VIOLA. Now get that child into my camp. Go on now git...

MAN IN ROBE. Yes ma'am.

> *(KKK Man darts off.)*

BEN. Fix'n to get us killed with that shotgun, woman?

VIOLA. Damn site better than the influenza I reckon...

> *(***JUAN JOSÉ*** *pokes at the KKK garb with a twig.)*

JUAN JOSÉ. She just save my life.

VIOLA. Who he?

BEN. Never laid eyes on him before...

VIOLA. Who you boy? You sick? You need Viola castor oil?

JUAN JOSÉ. I cannot afford your oil *porque* I have no Obamacare.

BEN. What the hell is *that?*

VIOLA. Ben, this here boy might be touched, soft about the head like.

BEN. Soft about the head?

VIOLA. Uh huh...

BEN. You soft about the head boy!?

(**JUAN JOSÉ** *touches his head to check for softness.*)

Best just move on down the road hombre.

VIOLA. We could use another hand Ben.

(**VIOLA** *quickly reaches into the tent and drags the end of a wrapped corpse slightly out of the tent.*)

BEN. You know how to plow a field boy?

JUAN JOSÉ. No. But I will Google it.

BEN. He no use to us.

VIOLA. Come here boy, fetch this here end of Mr. Johnson. Take him down to the willows. Bury him up but real good now. Go on. Both you. *Ándale* now!

(**BEN** *and* **JUAN JOSÉ** *quickly grab Mr. Johnston.*)

Don't forget the lime Mr. Ben.

BEN. We all but out of lime Miss Viola.

VIOLA. Don't trifle with me now. Got no time for it.

(*Removing his cowboy hat for moment to wipe his bald-head.*)

BEN. Yes ma'am. You heard the lady.

JUAN JOSÉ. Yessir. I not trifle. How the Mr. Johnson he die?

BEN. Spanish Lady got 'em. Just like all the rest...

JUAN JOSÉ. A Spanish Lady?

BEN. Influenza, Spanish Flu, I call it The Black Plague...

(**JUAN JOSÉ** *drops his end of Mr. Johnson.*)

Lucky die quick. Yessir. A killer has hit West Texas with a wallop.

JUAN JOSÉ. I cannot die before my big US test tomorrow!
BEN. Suit yourself…

> *(KKK Man re-enters with baby.)*

MAN IN ROBE. Miss Viola! Here be baby Jessup…
VIOLA. Oh Lord… What have we got here?

> *(KKK Man's infant is in head to toe baby-klan wear.)*

> *(VIOLA holds it aloft the way all mothers inspect babies.)*

MAN IN ROBE. Is *that* the corpse of Mister Johnson?
VIOLA. Yessir. More hot water Mexican boy!
JUAN JOSÉ. More hot water, more hot water? Suddenly I am the water boy? *Chingow* my dream is starting to suck a little bit.

> *(JUAN JOSÉ moves toward the Judge and the fema water bucket.)*

Señor Judge, do you know who are the Original Thirteen Colonies?

MAN IN ROBE. Sure. Everything south of the Mason Dixon Line, boy.
JUAN JOSÉ. Oh snap…

> *(JJ checks his little US pocket study book.)*

BEN. Coffee for ya Judge?
MAN IN ROBE. Never took coffee with no Nigger before.
BEN. That makes two of us…

> *(Men sit with coffee. JUAN JOSÉ and cards. Crickets.)*

Question for you Judge… Do y'all wives ever complain about all they fancy bedding gone missing? They fine linens and Egyptian cottons riding buck wild, terrorizing the countryside?

> *(Judge considers this. VIOLA can be heard from her tent:)*

VIOLA. Keep Viola castor oil down child... Swallow baby.

MAN IN ROBE. Ben, there's talk. Men in town, they're fixing to form a riding party...

BEN. What they be need'n a posse for Judge?

MAN IN ROBE. They aim to run y'all outta Brewster County for tending to the Mexicans.

JUAN JOSÉ. The Mexicans?

BEN. They got no call to run us off.

MAN IN ROBE. I'm just a messenger Ben...

BEN. We already but outta town, Judge.

MAN IN ROBE. To which is why you shall take Viola's camp more west...

BEN. Hardly no west left *in* West Texas.

(Somebody has entered camp.)

*(**MAN IN ROBE** points his lugar at the intruders.)*

Steady now fellas. Everybody stay calm...

(A and woman with a small baby bundle stumble into camp like already dead troops of Zapata's Army.)

*(**MEXICAN MAN** wears dusty Top Hat with long black coat and bullet Bandoleers across his chest – he's just left Pancho Villa's Northern Regiments.)*

*(His **WOMAN** is a Railroad Woman or rialera – she wears her own Bandoleers and carries the barely alive baby.)*

MEXICAN WOMAN. *Por favor, ayúdanos. Por favor señor.*

MEXICAN MAN. We just cross The River *señores...*

MEXICAN WOMAN. Our baby, Juan Josécito, he esleeping too much.

MAN IN ROBE. More wets crossing at The Lower Rio Grande?

MEXICAN MAN. Only the three of us *señor...*

MAN IN ROBE. It's a *Goddamned* invasion! (*darting look to* **JUAN JOSÉ**)

MEXICAN MAN. *¡No señor!*

BEN. Juan José! Show this here woman into Viola tent.

JUAN JOSÉ. But I must study my US civic book right now!

MEXICAN MAN. *¡Ándale joven!*

MEXICAN WOMAN. *Ayúdanos muchacho!*

> (**JUAN JOSÉ** *makes a move toward the tent.*)

MAN IN ROBE. I will not allow a wetback child in that tent!

> (**VIOLA** *emerges from the tent.*)

VIOLA. Stand down Judge! Gimme the child…

> (*The* **MEXICAN WOMAN** *hands baby to* **VIOLA**: *the child wears a sombrero and small baby bandoliers. He is held aloft.*)

Oh Lord what we have here?

> (*Inspecting just as she did the KKK Baby.*)

BEN. Nothing we can do now Judge 'cept let the woman do what she do. Viola in charge now.

MAN IN ROBE. (*disgust*) What sort of man let a woman run his camp?

BEN. Smart man do.

> (*From inside* **VIOLA** *quickly places an "OCUPADO" sign on the outside tent door flap and hums her soft healing songs.*)

> (**JUAN JOSÉ** *is drawn to the* **MEXICAN MAN**:)

JUAN JOSÉ. (*not sure*) I know you *señor*…

MEXICAN MAN. This is not possible *amigo*.

JUAN JOSÉ. *No señor,* I do know you.

MEXICAN MAN. Stand away from me *cabrón*…

JUAN JOSÉ. You have the little mark – there – like my papa… The teardrop mole… Right there…

> (**JUAN JOSÉ** *gently touches a mole under his eye.*)

> (**MEXICAN MAN** *swiftly snatches* **JUAN JOSÉ** *hand.*)

JUAN JOSÉ. What is your name soldier?

MEXICAN MAN. (*tossing hand down*) I am Juan José.

JUAN JOSÉ. No way José! That is my name too…

MEXICAN MAN. I am Juan José the Number One. *El Primero, cabrón.*

JUAN JOSÉ. I swear to God I do know you…

> (**MEXICAN MAN** *reaches into* **JJ***'s shirt pocket.*)

MEXICAN MAN. What the hell is this you carry here?

JUAN JOSÉ. My Constitution of the United States pocket book…

MEXICAN MAN. Declaration *de Independencia*, USA? *Mierda!* (*shit!*)

> (*He tosses the booklet into fire.*)

JUAN JOSÉ. Hey I *need* that!

> (**JJ** *tries to pick it up.*)

MAN IN ROBE. That wasn't very neighborly of you. Tossing our sacred history book into the fire.

JUAN JOSÉ. I agree with you Judge.

MEXICAN MAN. You and your little book can burn in the hell with the activist judge there…

BEN. Sure do hate you some white man.

MAN IN ROBE. White man hate *him* right back.

JUAN JOSÉ. *Mucho* haters here…

BEN. Let me pour you some coffee Juan José the First…

MAN IN ROBE. I gotta take coffee with a wetback now too?

MEXICAN MAN. I never drink coffee with crackers before…

JUAN JOSÉ. *Oh E-*snap!

BEN. Come up Big Bend you say?

MEXICAN MAN. Big Bend. *Sí señor.* Three nights hiding in the rocks. Crossing the river. Switchbacks, hounds on the trail, white men on horses with the big guns, the Night Riders, Los Texas Rangers behind us always...

We start in Gila Bend to *Piedras Negras* all the way to Eagle Pass. Three nights sleeping in the cave with the baby, three nights in the cold cave with the *nene!*

JUAN JOSÉ. *(referring to self) Como la cuaresma.* Forty days walking in the desert yo.

> (VIOLA *emerging from the tent with a wrapped babe.*)

VIOLA. Sound like the Holy Ghost Time to me... *Jesus Cristo...*

MEXICAN MAN. *En el otro lado,* on the *other* side, they say Miss Viola is here, *en su gloria,* mi *Ángel Negra. Gracias a Dios for this Benjamin...*

> (*With a nod and permission from the* MEXICAN MAN *places a gentle kiss on the over worked hand of* VIOLA.)

VIOLA. Do they really say that?

MEXICAN MAN. *Sí señora.*

VIOLA. I like it!

JUAN JOSÉ. I hear *this* before...

VIOLA. Mexican Boy, come do mama's toes and corns...

JUAN JOSÉ. Surgical mask?

BEN. Yonder by the FEMA bucket son.

> (JUAN JOSÉ *lifts up a surgical mask and enters the tent.*)

MAN IN ROBE. You one of Pancho Villa's *bandidos* ain't ya?

MEXICAN MAN. *(proudly) Bandido no. I am Soldado. De División: Batallón 30/30.*

> (*Surgically Masked* JJ *popping out from tent.*)

JUAN JOSÉ. So was my great grandfather!

MEXICAN MAN. I am from the North Garrison. Armored Division. Fighting against your Black-Jack Pershing.

(The Black-Jack sounds punctuated like an intended insult.)

MAN IN ROBE. Why you wear them Injun braids and top hat for boy? Got some prairie Nigga in ya?

(Mexican-Man rises slowly for the inevitable. Crickets.)

MEXICAN MAN. I am multi-cultural *señor*. I am *fashionista* and Desert Dandy. This is how I roll. My Papa is known as *El Comanche de Chihuahua, cabrón.*

JUAN JOSÉ. *(penny dropping)* My people are from Chihuahua too…

MEXICAN MAN. *No manches guey…*

MAN IN ROBE. Your Villa and Zapata must have forgotten the ass whooping ya'll took at the Treaty of Guadalupe Hidalgo?

MEXICAN MAN. We not forget about this amigo, but we prefer to remember The Alamo with great delight!

MAN IN ROBE. I lost kin at San Antone you greasy river rat!

MEXICAN MAN. *So did I* Jimmy Crow! Andale!

(Quick as light they draw on each other.)

JUAN JOSÉ. I just sign the Treaty of Guadalupe Hidalgo moments ago.

*(***MEXICAN MAN*** *aims and cocks a second gun at* ***JUAN JOSÉ.***)*

MEXICAN MAN. Traitor.

MAN IN ROBE. *(defending* **JJ***)* Hero.

JUAN JOSÉ. I would like a Mexican Coca Cola now…

BEN. *(rising with real concern)* Got us a real Mexican standoff out here Viola!

JUAN JOSÉ. I am sickening and tired of all these guns in *my* dream!

*(***MEXICAN MAN*** *slowly cocks his gun at KKK Man – more danger.)*

MEXICAN MAN. And what will you do about then *bastardo?*

JUAN JOSÉ. Well, in my knapsack I have a dead bunny that the Jewish Chino Hip Hop gringo guy give me for lunch, I will twirl him aloft with deadly force maybe...

> (*JUAN JOSÉ is reaching and making this up as he goes.*)

BEN. The hell you say...

> (*In a flash of light* JJ *has just that – twirling a bunny!*)

MAN IN ROBE. Look out he's got the bunny!

> (*JJ deftly twirls the furry like a pair of lethal nunchucks.*)

MEXICAN MAN. *¡Ay cabrón!*

JUAN JOSÉ. *(Tony Montana)* Say hello to my furry little friend!

> (*JJ kicks like 70' Kung Foo movie and funky wa-wa-porn guitar.*)

MEXICAN MAN. *The freaky furry bunny escare me!*

ALL. Estop! Estop! Estop!

> (*The men surrender their guns in a trance like state at the feet of* JUAN JOSÉ.)

> (*Lights and calm are restored.*)

> (**VIOLA** *pops her head out from the tent:*)

VIOLA. *(awe)* Well then, the Man swings a mean bunny.

> (*The men agree.* MEXICAN MAN *has laid all weapons at* JJ*'s feet.*)

Y'all keep the conversation polite or you'll be on your way!

ALL. *Yes ma'am. Sí Señora...*

BEN. Keep them irons holstered now fellas...

JUAN JOSÉ. Now, if you don't mind I'm going to study my flash cards in peace and quiet next to the rotting corpse of Mr. Johnson. Who will help me?

(ALL eager to help JJ now. MEXICAN MAN grabs US Flashcard:)

MEXICAN MAN. I help you, I help you Juan Josecito. *Bueno,* civic flashcard question *numero* Trece: Name *eh* the three...uh...what is this word gringo?

MAN IN ROBE. Branches...

MEXICAN MAN. *Gracias cabrón.* Where are your *pantalones?* Never mind.

> *(KKK Man is slightly vulnerable and self-conscious.)*

Bueno, name three of branches of the United States Government *por favor, Juan Josesito?*

JUAN JOSÉ. Ah *bueno* Juan Jose The Number 1, you pick a hard one man.

MEXICAN MAN. *Oh sí...* *(so pleased with himself)*

JUAN JOSÉ. OKAY: The Executive, the Legislative and the Judicial!

> *(MEXICAN MAN throws the cards down.)*

MEXICAN MAN. I hate your government!

MAN IN ROBE. I hate my government too!

> *(Momentary surprise that the man have one thing in common.)*

MEXICAN MAN. You are extreme Calvinist perhaps?

MAN IN ROBE. No. Hare Krishna.

MEXICAN MAN. I have no money... I have no money.

> *(Hands held aloft in surrender MEXICAN MAN rises away from KKK Man as if he were a leper. The men reposition around the fire.)*

> *(ALL quiet and tense again. Crickets fart gently in the Night.)*

> *(BEN tries to ease the pungent air.)*

BEN. Let's see here, uh, so, a Colored Cowboy, a Mexican Revolutionary and a Klan Judge all walk into a saloon...

(BEN loses joke steam – the men are completely lost and silent.)

There's a joke in there somewhere. Hell if I know where 'tis.

(Beat. Explosive laughter. VIOLA emerges from the tent.)

VIOLA. Y'all having your fun and games out here?
BEN. Uh...
VIOLA. You got more jokes Mister Ben?
BEN. No ma'am... We're miserable out here...
VIOLA. Uh huh.

(MISS VIOLA moves to the Judge.)

Judge, your baby gone be fine. She strong.
MAN IN ROBE. God bless you Viola...
VIOLA. Never mind the blessing ya'll need to leave now.
MAN IN ROBE. Yes ma'am.
VIOLA. Your baby too Mexican Man, he okay...
MEXICAN MAN. *Gracias a Dios for this Viola.*

(VIOLA darts back into the tent.)

Our babies are going to live. Thanks be to God. *(sign of the cross)* Your baby too Señor Judge.

(MEXICAN MAN and KKK Man slowly move toward each other awkward.)

This is good...
MAN IN ROBE. Si...

(MEXICAN and KKK Man are over come with relief and gratitude and are very close if not face to face.)

(They offer a quick strike hard slap/hug and push away release as violent as it might be comforting.)

(KKK Man moves to JJ and offers another pocket size book.)

MAN IN ROBE. Here you go Johnny-Joe, take this, my pappy's travel bible, Exalted Cyclops of all Texas he was.

JUAN JOSÉ. El Cyclops? *Qué honor...*

> (**MEXICAN MAN** *tosses* **JJ** *his own Red Book from across the rock.*)

MEXICAN MAN. *Mijo!* Better you should take my little Red Book...

JUAN JOSE. *(reading)* The Communist Manifesto?

MEXICAN MAN. *Sí señor.* With a wonderful foreword by Rachel Maddow.

> (*Just then two US Cavalry Men enter the camp. Trumpet!*)

LT. SEGUIN. United States Cavalry! Lieutenant Seguin. We've been tracking this man since he crossed into The Territory.

MEXICAN MAN. No señor!

OFFICER BLANCHARD. Our orders are to roundup all Mexicans from the skirmish line!

JUAN JOSÉ. But I be *Americano mañana...*

MEXICAN MAN. *(protecting* **JJ***) Cállate Juan Josesito!*

OFFICER BLANCHARD. *(dizzy-sick)* I command you in the name of... Oh God I gotta get in that tent...

> (**BLANCHARD** *falls back into tent with violent loose bowels.*)

> (**MEXICAN MAN** *bolts!*)

MEXICAN MAN. *¡Viva Villa! ¡Mi caballo! Run Juan José!*

> (**MEXICAN MAN** *flees.* **LT. SEGUIN** *gives hi-step Victorian chase.*)

LT. SEGUIN. Halt, sexy Mexican Man! Halt I say!

> (*Shots fired.* **VIOLA** *steps from out of the tent with KKK Baby.*)

VIOLA. Take the child home now Judge!

(KKK Man offers **BEN** *something moving him away from the Women.)*

MAN IN ROBE. Take this Ben.

BEN. Your prized Luger Judge? *(reluctant)*

MAN IN ROBE. Be wise to grab hold of her.

> *(**BEN** takes hold if it slow and unsure.)*

For the hounds or them Night Riders. Who ever come first.

> *(A rare and generous gesture as the conflicted Judge exits.)*

> *(Coyotes answer Dogs in the distance. **BEN** studies the Lugar.)*

BEN. Whole lotta hate and heat in West Texas.

VIOLA. You fix'n to get us killed with his honors gun, Mister Ben?

BEN. Better me than the influenza I reckon...

VIOLA. *(rare weariness)* Good Lord carry me another night...

BEN. Good Lord all but forgot about West Texas.

JUAN JOSÉ. *(looking at Almanac)* History forget about West Texas too...

VIOLA. What'chu be talken 'bout now boy?

JUAN JOSÉ. I don't read anything about Miss Viola or Señor Ben in my US history book, no pictures. *Nada!*

VIOLA. They don't write about no daughters of sharecroppers in the important history books, son.

BEN. My people came off the slave ships in Galveston Bay, worked every cotton gin from here to Corpus.

JUAN JOSÉ. The Cotton's is here for sure *Señor* Ben.

BEN. 'Cause cotton be King in Texas boy.

VIOLA. And I *do* not Worship Kings.

JUAN JOSÉ. I reckon it is so. *(recently learned lingo) But...*

> *(**JUAN JOSÉ** begins to write directly in his book.)*

Never a day too bad or Night too dark that Viola Canada Pettus won't go where needed... Where there is sickness. Viola be there for sure. Okay, I just write you into American History.

VIOLA. I felt that very much. *Muchas gracias señor.*

JUAN JOSÉ. You are great lady Miss Viola. Like an American Angel.

VIOLA. God ain't give me wings yet. I'll let you know if he do.

> *(trains in the distance.)*

> *(Bucket with fema writ bold on it rolls out of the tent.)*

MEXICAN WOMAN. *(head through tent)* The Soldier, he just kick the bucket.

VIOLA. Another soul has flown!

> *(The Dead Soldier brings new danger for all they move swift:)*

BEN. Best get him in the ground before the coyote's catch his scent. Damn hound dogs be circling us soon too!

> *(Coyotes in the distance.)*

VIOLA. Juan Jose y'all best get up out this camp right now. Come here son, you gone have to escort this here woman and the child back across the *Rio Grande.*

JUAN JOSÉ. No, no, I just *leave* Mexico Miss Viola. I never go back.

VIOLA. Don't trifle with me now boy... Listen to Viola...

JUAN JOSÉ. But I have citizenship test in just a couple of hours...

BEN. Juan José you're not safe here and that's a fact.

JUAN JOSE. *(continues to protest)* I go North now then *Señor* Ben!

> *(BEN's words and firm arm quickly pull JJ downstage.)*

BEN. Look here son, every county jail from Hidalgo to Huntsville is plumb full-up, and who you think be sitten up in them jails boy? Mexicans be Mexicans.

VIOLA. Women, children, babies too...

JUAN JOSÉ. But I not *those* people.

BEN. In West Texas you *are* those people.

JUAN JOSÉ. But I will be American soon you will see, Señor Ben!

VIOLA. *(real urgency)* Time be a'wasting. Set out now son it's your only hope.

MEXICAN WOMAN. We need to move now!

VIOLA. *Hasta pronto...*

> *(VIOLA places the Infant in JUAN JOSÉ's. The Baby cries.)*

JUAN JOSÉ. Why you cry? No cry... Do I know you little guy?

> *(The Baby stops crying and is now cooing.)*

What is this baby boy? You have *un lunar,* the *lágrima* under your eye little teardrop mole just like your *papá...*

MEXICAN WOMAN. And his *Papá...*

JUAN JOSÉ. Who are you *mijo?*

MEXICAN WOMAN. You very much like him... The Teardrop...

JUAN JOSÉ. My Mother used to tell us a story just before bedtime...

> *(We hear VIOLA's wind chimes recorded at the Marathon Cemetery.)*

MEXICAN WOMAN. About the Black Woman in the North who save many Mexican Families...
Our *familia...*

JUAN JOSÉ. *(looking at child)* This mean...

> *(A beat as JUAN JOSÉ looks to her at the astonishment of it.)*

VIOLA. *(calm)* Don't drop him...

(JJ *goes to his knees with the improbable weight of the Child.*)

JUAN JOSÉ. *Tú eres mi otro yo.* You Are My Other Self.

(JUAN JOSÉ *lifting the baby up ever skyward.*)

Abuelo! (Grandfather)

(MEXICAN WOMAN *walks to* JJ *and places a hand on his forehead.*)

MEXICAN WOMAN. Let me bless you *and* your grandfather...

JUAN JOSÉ. *Thank you* Great Grandmother...

(JJ *looks up to her in gentle rapture and surrender.*)

(BEN *grabs his cowboy hat from the rock as he and* VIOLA *too "lay hands" on* JUAN JOSÉ.)

(*Negro Spiritual Hymnal voices from a hundred years ago mix with Mexican Catholicism and border Indio mysticism at the redemptive and blood-rooted waters of West Texas.*)

(*http://www.negrospirituals.com/news-song/deep_river.htm*)

(*"Crossing the River Jordan" or "Deep River" have nice reverberations to crossing the Rio Grande...* As:)

MEXICAN WOMAN. *(soft spoke prayer)*
Ángel de mi guarda,
Dulce companía,
Ne me desampares,
Ni de dia, Ni de noche,
Dios conmigo, Yo con El...
Ángel de mi guarda...

(*The Benediction inspires* JJ *lifting him into action.*)

JUAN JOSÉ. Okay. I take you across the border safely baby boy!

BEN. *(proudly)* There's my young buck!

> *(Hear the paleta cart bells [ice scream cart] of*
> **DOÑA TENCHA** *the ice cream Woman from* **JJ**'s
> *Mexican pueblo.)*

Somebody coming this way…

DOÑA TENCHA. *Hielito… Hielito…*

JUAN JOSÉ. It is Dona Tencha from my *pueblo!*

MEXICAN WOMAN. She made for him every day his favorite
hielo?

JUAN JOSÉ. The lemon ice I love so much… You want
lemon snow little guy?

> (**DONA TENCHA** *pushes her ice cream cart toward*
> *them.)*

DOÑA TENCHA. *Lemoncito para mi Juan Josécito, claro que sí…*

> *(She opens a hatch on top of the cart which*
> *emanates light:)*

> *(She hands out large yellow snow cones of lemon*
> *ice.)*

Lemoncito, para mis Negritos lindos…

> *(Yellow ice cones for the eager hands of* **VIOLA** *and*
> **BEN**.*)*

VIOLA. *Gracias Doña Tencha!*

> *(Just then a posse, horses, guns and hounds are*
> *heard off stage:)*

Gone get me some Niggas!

Send out those Mexicans Ben Pettus!

Posse Comitatus gone get you too Viola! Heya!

> (**ALL** *move swift:* **JJ** *places the and her)*

> *(Baby on the front end of the ice cream cart as:)*

JUAN JOSÉ. I will stay here for my test, you must go with
Doña Tencha, she will carry you both safely across the
River!

(JJ *lifts onto the ice cream cart with Baby.*)

Ándale! Move swift like the Santa Fe!

(*Shotguns and horses are heard.*)

(**DOÑA TENCHA** *hums and quickly exits with the Family.*)

(**BEN** *and* **VIOLA** *exit swift looking like a Kara Walker silhouette.*)

(*Night and chaos continue to fall on West Texas.*)

(*The Tent descends down into the trap or moved off.*)

(*We hear* **VIOLA***'s Marathon cemetery wind chimes as:*)

(*Transition: moving train projections and sounds.*)

(*A Tumbleweed moves across upstage.*)

(*Two* **HOBOS** *enter to break a new camp.*)

(*At this time we must hear echoes of* **MISTER WOODY GUTHRIE:**)

"This Land is your land, this land is my land..."*

(**HOBO 1 AND 2** *move in close to* **JUAN JOSÉ** *– there is a "conversation" though less important than the kind gesture shown to a stranger in The Night.*)

(**HOBO 2** *hands* **JJ** *a much-needed flask with fresh water.*)

HOBO 2. How do son? This here is Mister Woody Guthrie son. Show your respects, now.

JUAN JOSÉ. How do *señores?*

(**WOODY** *tips his hat as* **JJ** *drinks from flask.*)

WOODY. (*hushed*) Never let 'em fence you in son...

JUAN JOSÉ. Okay Woody...

WOODY. See you boys up at Hopper Ranch then...

HOBO 2. ...With the Timber Fallers!

> (**WOODY** *shuffles off with his guitar strapped on his back.*)

> (*As The West Texas Tent goes away the* **HOBOS** *serve to gracefully move off the camp fire and rock left by* **HOP LING** *and others.*)

> (**HOBOS** *are joined by a third all move on leaving an empty stage*)

> (*As four old timey microphones [1940s] rise up from the floor.*)

> (*Hear: "Moonlight serenade"**)

> (**MANZANAR** *Japanese Internment Center!*)

> (*Projections: black and white images of:*)

> (*US Japanese internment camps: Young Women Smiling* –)

> (*American Japanese Americans loaded on trains* –)

> (*Faces of hopeful children waving US American flags* –)

> (*Proud to be American signs in a Japanese Store* –)

> (**JUAN JOSÉ** *watches the images in amazement* –)

> (*An elegant* **ANGLO MAN** *enters in herringbone suit and fedora.*)

> (*He reads in an easy-breezy style from his yellow radio pages:*)

RADIO ANNOUNCER. It's time for The Camp Manzanar Radio Theater Hour!

> (*A Foley Man works sound cues at a Foley Table that slides in.*)

---

*Please see Music Use Note on page 3

Broadcasting live from the gymnasium of the Manzanar Reloca-tion Center – a modern marvel of safety and cleanliness near Lone Pine California…

(Foley Man: Wolf howl.)

…Nestled deep in the rustic Owens Valley and available on your short wave radio dial, today's program is sponsored by the United States Department of Defense. Remember, Good Americans buy US War Bonds! Why Uncle Sam is counting on you.

Today's broadcast is also brought to you by Lucky Strike Cigarettes: every cigarette a fine cylinder of fresh, mild tobacco delivering rich flavor deep into your lungs – get the honest taste of Lucky Strike!

(Foley Man holds up a Lucky Strike Sign and coughs on his fag.)

The Manzanar Radio Players are played by actual residents of the camp. Appearing in the role of Donut Shop Delivery Man will be special guest-worker: *Juan José.*

(The Foley Man quickly holds up an applause sign then helps dress **JUAN JOSÉ** *with paper envelope hat, apron and donut box.)*

*(***JJ*** *awkwardly stands near a microphone.)*

And now, tonight's episode of "The Unusual Mexican-American Teenage Camp Guest": here's Young Ralf Lazo everybody…

(The word "everybody" is key to understanding the 1940s vernacular of US radio speak. It is elongated and elegant. Every syllable is enjoyed.)

(Enter **RALF LAZO***: a real hep-cat in a light waste jacket and baggy wool pants. He wears an old newsboy cap like* **WOODY GUTHRIE** *would have.)*

(There are no scripts for the actors of the Radio Play.)

(This troupe of camp actors performs every Saturday night for the camp detainees – though tonight's show may be different:)

RALF. What-a-ya-say Donut Man?

JUAN JOSÉ. What do I say Donut Man?

RALF. Yeah. What-a-ya-say?

JUAN JOSÉ. The man just say I am the Donut Delivery Man. It is my dream job. You want glazed or old-fashioned?

RALF. Got a Lucky Strike for a wayward youth?

JUAN JOSÉ. *Híjole* Ralfie, this Manzanar internment camp it is a prison?

RALF. It's not a Kibbutz summer camp, kid.

JUAN JOSÉ. Why are *you* here man?

RALF. Why I put myself here.

JUAN JOSÉ. You give up your freedom Ralfie?

RALF. Why all my Japanese friends from high school are here or up Tule Lake see?

JUAN JOSÉ. But you are Chicano from LA el Ralfie...

RALF. Sure some squares think it's queer for a Mex kid from East LA to be up here with the Japanese, I say it's wrong for them to be here and *not* me! *(painful memory not cartoon)* Are you *red* Ralf Lazo they asked? Are you Un-American Ralf Lazo they said.

JUAN JOSÉ. And what did you say El Ralfie?

RALF. I told 'em I came to Manzanar because I *am* American.

JUAN JOSÉ. You have very large *huevos* Ralfie.

RALF. I was born with a large *huevos* Donut Man.

JUAN JOSÉ. *Pos sí...*

RALF. I grew up with the Japanese folk in the neighborhood see. Buddha Heads as far as the eye could see. Like family see.

JUAN JOSÉ. *Pos sí...*

RALF. Why when they were rounded up from their homes, they weren't doing nothun wrong: Why Mrs. Watanabe was tending her reefer garden and Mr. Yamada was in his store refusing to serve the Negroes just like other regular Americans...

JUAN JOSÉ. You stand up for your *amigos*. I see this so nice. Maybe one day I can be a good American just like you El Ralfie.

RALF. Don't pop a boner pal.

> *(Foley Man: Boing SQ.)*

> *(Enter Camp Teacher* MRS. FINNEY *with "String of Pearls":)*

Why it's perky camp teacher Mrs. Finney!

> *(Foley Man with an applause sign:)*

MRS. FINNEY. Say who's the pleasant Mexican fella?

RALF. Say hey to the new Donut Man, he's dreaming right now.

MRS. FINNEY. It's a free country I suppose.

JUAN JOSÉ. Yes, and I estudy the FDR and the "Four Freedoms" and this stick in my *cabeza* and now I here with you I think...

MRS. FINNEY. Why that makes perfect sense.

JUAN JOSÉ. And then I was in the *Hunger Games* with Saca-Chihuahua...

MRS. FINNEY. Oh prison guard!

JUAN JOSÉ. Perhaps you can help me with my flash cards Mrs. Finney. I bet you are a good teacher.

> *(*JUAN JOSÉ *gives* MRS. FINNEY *the Flash Cards.)*

Toma ask me a question, anything I answer. Go for it!

MRS. FINNEY. Why these flash cards are in Swahili, see?

> *(*MRS. FINNEY *drops the cards and laughs slightly spooky.)*

> *(*JJ *scrambles to pick up his cards with a slight panic.)*

JUAN JOSÉ. My dream is sucking again.

(Enter JOHNNY YAMAMORI.)

(JOHNNY wears zoot suit pants, leather bomber jacket, tight white T-shirt, cross and a chain he can swing from his pocket.)

(His shoes are as black as his bad ass Pachuco pompadour with D.A. Tail on the back of his doo.)

(JOHNNY is the Camp Bad Ass but with a good and fair heart.)

(A smoldering Japanese Brando before Brando of the '40s.)

RALF. Say its Johnny Yamamori!

JOHNNY. Hello everybody.

> *(JOHNNY and RALF sound as American as MRS. FINNEY.)*

MRS. FINNEY. How are you Johnny?

JOHNNY. Good as you and twice as fresh Mrs. Finney.

> *(JOHNNY combs his hair with his own sound cue from Foley Man.)*

MRS. FINNEY. Oh Johnny now...

RALF. You're the coolest *vato* in camp Johnny-boy.

JOHNNY. *Arigato ese vato...*

RALF. Say hey to Juan José.

JOHNNY. What'ya say what'ya know Donut Man?

> *(reading his cards from the ground)*

JUAN JOSÉ. My flash cards are in Aramaic...?

JOHNNY. *(super cool)* Crazy daddy-o... You wanna join our jacket club Donut Man?

JUAN JOSÉ. *¿Qué qué?*

JOHNNY/RALF. *(super cool)* The Manzanar Knights!

> *(JOHNNY and RALF spin on cue revealing cool jacket logos:)*

JUAN JOSÉ. *Chido* man. I never join anything in America.

MRS. FINNEY. Why that's very nice of you boys to ask the Mexican to join your summer youth gang.

JUAN JOSÉ. I am in Johnny's Gang! *Órale...*

ALL. *Órale!*

> *(The all lean back like Pachucos.* **MRS. FINNEY** *catches herself:)*

MRS. FINNEY. *(recovering)* Perhaps we should be cautious with the rough barrio street language kids?

JUAN JOSÉ. *Híjole* Johnny, can you teach me the American jitterbug?

JOHNNY. Not a pepper-shaker myself kid but a drape shape is banaroo...

> *(***JOHNNY*** *leans back all Pachuco cool.)*

JUAN JOSÉ. Jeepers creepers I like these crazy American words!

JOHNNY. Say Donut Man, help us sneak off camp tonight?

RALF. Sure JJ, you could be our outside man see?

JUAN JOSÉ. *Sí.*

MRS. FINNEY. Boys you know I can't let you off camp tonight.

JOHNNY/RALF. Ah man...

MRS. FINNEY. Why if you got caught you'll miss all your lessons.

JOHNNY. *(simmering streak of fatalism)* Only the trout get caught Mrs. Finney. Their bloody mouths agape, their gills ripped from the rusty hooks at the end of Mister Kishi's bamboo pole.

MRS. FINNEY. Why that's an unpleasant and violent image Johnny.

JOHNNY. Why it's an unpleasant and violent world Mrs. Finney.

MRS. FINNEY. *(not musicalized)* In this classroom we *will* accentuate the positive...

JUAN JOSÉ. I am Mister In Between? *(quietly realizing)*

JOHNNY. I'm so mad at Mr. Roosevelt right now. FUBAR on his damn Executive Order ninety-sixty-six. *Ano bakatre ga!*

RALF. *So da, so da!*

MRS. FINNEY. Easy with the Kamikaze language. English *only* fellas.

JUAN JOSÉ. English only? I hear this before…

JOHNNY. Pops is really sore at Roosevelt too. But Father says we must hide our anger deep down inside, show no emotion. The older *Hapo* folks are frightened, the guard told them they're all getting deported back to Japan.

JUAN JOSÉ. But you are born in America el Johnny-boy?

JOHNNY. Good Sam Hospital. City of Angels.

JUAN JOSÉ. The government can put innocent citizens in a cage like this?

MRS. FINNEY. Don't you have more deliveries, Donut Man?

JUAN JOSÉ. What kind of America put in prison her own *gente?*

MRS. FINNEY. A War-time America does. A frightened America does. A country that was attacked without warning. Every Precaution must be taken to protect her shores whether we are fond of it or not.

JOHNNY. Precautions Mrs. Finney? Precautions against the sick baby girl, born this morning at Heart Mountain internment camp? Jap babies hatched like Koi fish in a white man's pond. Baby Catherine is her name, after the Quaker Lady who visits us every single day.

JUAN JOSÉ. *(reading)* It says right here in my pocket book: "The right of the people to be secure in their persons, houses, papers, and effects, against unreasonable searches and seizures…" This is the Fourth Amendment, no?

JOHNNY. No Bill of Rights at Manzanar Donut Man…

RALF. Amen to that brother.

MRS. FINNEY. Now fellas, let's try our level best to do as we rehearsed.

JOHNNY. Easy for you to say eh Mrs. Finney?

MRS. FINNEY. Look here I have to live in the same bitter cold the same dust storms stirring up the same Valley Fever and use the same smelly latrines as everybody else.

JOHNNY. But you don't *have* to be here Mrs. Finney.

RALF. Say Johnny ease up a bit will ya...

JOHNNY. Where's Mr. Finney I wonder?

MRS. FINNEY. I don't think that's any of your concern.

JOHNNY. What if I make it my concern?

MRS. FINNEY. I don't think you're being very kind at all.

JOHNNY. Where's the old man teach?

MRS. FINNEY. Mr. Finney is fighting the Japs.

> (*Everything comes to a halt. Foley Man scratches a record.*)

Oh my...

JOHNNY. Fighting the Jap's Mrs. Finney?

MRS. FINNEY. I don't remember that word in the script...

JOHNNY. The script's no good kid.

MRS. FINNEY. (*some pride*) Mr. Finney is proudly serving his country in the Pacific Theater.

JOHNNY. And you *teach* the Japs. Why?

MRS. FINNEY. Because...

JOHNNY. Because why?

MRS. FINNEY. Because nearly three thousand school children were brought to Manzanar with absolutely no plan to educate them and that angers me. It angers me a great deal if you must know. Does it anger you?

RALF/JUAN JOSÉ/JOHNNY. Hell yes!

MRS. FINNEY. It makes me plenty so.

JUAN JOSÉ. This is *good* Mrs. Finney...

MRS. FINNEY. I just don't go in for that sort of thing.

JOHNNY. You're pretty when you're cross Mrs. Finney.

MRS. FINNEY. Why pretty's got nothing to do with it. I'm terribly sorry I used that ugly word just now Johnny. There was no call for it...

JOHNNY. The day my big brother Tommy left for the war, when he joined up with the 4-42nd – why he said so long to me like he knew he was never coming back.

> *(Distant and respectful "taps" for a dead American soldier –)*

When mother received the telegram from the war saying he was dead, all I wanted to do was to be like him: Brave. Japanese-American. A fighter with the 4-42nd. *Go For Broke...* They said.

> *(Taps is gone.* **JOHNNY** *shifts to a quiet simmer of anger/shame.)*

Three days ago, they escorted my sister out of the University of California... Good Ol' CAL... Yanked her out like an unwanted weed in Mother's garden. 4.0 grade average, Glee Club, Miss All-American so she thought.

Marched out of Bolt Hall with the other Japanese kids like a Lotus Blossom parade – the entire student body pointing, laughing, frightened of her... They called her traitor and Tokyo Rose... I cannot imagine the shame sister must have felt...

JUAN JOSÉ. *(ever softly)* What is your sister's name Johnny?

JOHNNY. *Uriko...*

JUAN JOSÉ. *Uriko.* This is a beautiful name Johnny.

MRS. FINNEY. You have every reason to be cross with your country son but you can't give up on America you just can't.

JOHNNY. I wanted be a Tail Gunner, a bombardier, serve my country sure, but my country wants me to sign a loyalty oath first.

RALF. Me too. *(some hurt)*

JOHNNY. Maybe I'll join the No-No Boys.

JUAN JOSÉ. But you are loyal Americans man.

JOHNNY. Go tell it to Uncle Sam.

JUAN JOSÉ. How do you do it el Johnny? First you lose your *hermano* then your kid sister humiliated like this? I think you are my new American hero Johnny.

JOHNNY. I ain't no hero kid.

JUAN JOSÉ. Sure you are el Johnny. And I feel your *familia* very much...

> *(Hungry coyotes howl in the distance.* JOHNNY *is wistful.)*

JOHNNY. Sounds like Echo Park.

MRS. FINNEY. I've never been to Echo Park Johnny. Is it a desperate and lonely slum-barrio?

JOHNNY. It's okay I guess. Just miss it. Like I miss Nisei's Pool Parlor in J-Town with Tommy and Jackie and the Brooklyn Dodgers on Dad's transistor radio.

RALF. *(gentle)* Tommy was Aces Johnny.

JOHNNY. You're a good friend to every single person at Manzanar Ralf Lazo.

RALF. *Arigato ese vato...*

> *(Foley Man gently shakes a little ice cream cart bell.)*

JUAN JOSÉ. I miss the lemon snow and my wife in Mexico.

MRS. FINNEY. What else do you miss Johnny? What else?

JOHNNY. I miss summer nights at Sleepy Lagoon with my girl...

MRS. FINNEY. I miss mystery meat sandwiches on wonder bread with Miracle Whip.

> (ALL *look to* MRS. FINNEY:)

Híjole el Johnny. I'm over come with vapors. Kiss me!

JOHNNY. I'm coming in like a kamikaze Mrs. Finney!

MRS. FINNEY. Oh clear the decks of my SS UTAH El Johnny!

(Fighter Jet Dive Bomb sounds for big, forbidden movie kiss.)

*(**RADIO ANNOUNCER** rushes in to save the moment.)*

ANNOUNCER. Let us pause here for US War Bonds and a musical break with our very own Manzanar Madrigals! *A 1 a 2 a 3 a…*

(Fully orchestrated musical intro for "Don't Sit Under The Apple Tree" kick in:*)

*(Two Negroes with nice jackets and nice hair enter and gather round the **ANNOUNCER**'s mic and sing after intro:)*

MANZANAR MADRIGALS. *Don't sit under the apple tree with anyone else but me, Anyone else but me, anyone else but me, NO NO NO!*

*(**JOHNNY** dances with **MRS. FINNEY**.)*

*(**JJ** and **RALF** dance cool boogie-woogie style! Madrigals hum:)*

JUAN JOSÉ. You remind me of my wife el Ralfie.

RALF. This sure feels queer!

JUAN JOSÉ. Everything is loco! I want to be American but after I meet Johnny and the Japs, I'm not so sure… I'm not so sure…

(A WWII Air Raid Siren is heard as the dancing stops.)

ANNOUNCER. Guess they caught old man Kishi again, that old rascal.

(Bespectacled Old Man Kishi enters with a string of trout.)

MR. KISHI. *Koni chisa* fellas! *(Hello)*

ALL. Say Mr. Kishi!

---

*Please see Music Use Note on page 3

MR. KISHI. I just caught three trout! Three Golden Sierra Trout! Who want-a Sashimi?

MRS. FINNEY. Oh Mr. Kishi! What an adorable stereotype you are...

(Canned and cast laughter.)

MR. KISHI. Mr. Kishi not adorable stereotype! *(suddenly quiet)*

Mr. Kishi Yakuza! Yakuza with Haiku for Juan José-san. *Hay:*

(Ancient flutes:)

Crying child need –
Not same as crying child want –
Better to join both...

ANNOUNCER. Today's Haiku was sponsored by Atlantic Richfield service stations. Remember: Good Americans ration gasoline. This has been Radio Manzanar broadcasting from the Lone Pine area in California's Mojave Desert.

(A lone Wolf howl:)

Good night dear listeners and all our Ships at Sea!

ANNOUNCER/MR. KISHI. Hay!

*(Flute and deep Taiko Drum-like sounds as **JUAN JOSÉ** is now face to face with **MR. KISHI**.)*

*(As a sign of high respect **MR. KISHI** gently hands **JJ** his prized trout catch to go with the dead bunny: **JJ** bows and receives them as both bow respectful and ritualistically.)*

*(Cool Boy **JOHNNY** lingers up stage as **MR. KISHI** exits.)*

JOHNNY. So this is your dream eh kid?

JUAN JOSÉ. I think I lose control of my dream, but yes Johnny, it is mine...

JOHNNY. Then I wanna meet the Greatest American of all time.

JUAN JOSÉ. Nancy Pelosi?

JOHNNY. Na. Brooklyn Dodger Jackie Robinson. UCLA Bruin. All American.

JUAN JOSÉ. I don't know el Jackie el Johnny.

*(Crowd cheers and jeers as period Dodger **JACKIE ROBINSON** enters in vintage and accurate head to toe Dodger Blue. [Boo Giants!])*

JACKIE. Say…

JOHNNY. Say…

JACKIE. Wanna play toss Johnny?

JOHNNY. Sure I do Jackie…

*(They toss. **JUAN JOSÉ** watches and marvels.)*

Wow. Jackie Robinson. In Technicolor!

JACKIE. Say Johnny, I'll catch up with you later in the segregated showers after the game.

JOHNNY. What an honor. Sure Jackie. So long Donut Man. *Arigato ese vato!*

JUAN JOSÉ. *Órale el* Johnny.

(Both strike Pachuco pose as a appears.)

RABBI. Hello Jackie.

JACKIE. Hello Rabbi Green.

RABBI. Say Jackie, who's the *schvartza?*

JACKIE. Oh he's a traveler who wants to be an American.

RABBI. Looks thin, bring him for Friday dinner…

JACKIE. Yessir…

RABBI. Jackie I'm hearing things…

JACKIE. Like what Rabbi?

RABBI. Like O'Malley is gonna take the Bums West for instance! If that should happen it will be a *shanda* and Walter suffer testicular cancer! Peace be with you Jackie…

JACKIE. And also with you…

RABBI. Jackie turn off the lights at Temple on your way to Ebbets?

JACKIE. As always sir…

RABBI. You are a good Shabbos goy Jackie… *(RABBI exits)*

JUAN JOSÉ. I am a schvartza? That is an honor I think.

JACKIE. Take a knee son. Not everything is in your playbook. Not everything is in the playbill. Take my McGregor glove, go on son take a hold of her.

> *(JUAN JOSÉ reaches for the priceless glove:)*

Feel it's smooth leather. What does it say right there?

JUAN JOSÉ. Made in USA?

JACKIE. That's right. Flaws and all…

JUAN JOSÉ. I don't understand El Jackie…

> *(Ken Burns type documentary music – tasteful not funny.)*

JACKIE. Look here Juan José, one Night, there was a game, on the road near El Paso think it was, and I seen a sign, and the sign said: NO DOGS, NO NEGROES, NO MEXICANS.* In that order.

Now I see that sign, I believe that sign, even fear it, but I know that sign is not America. It is a part of it sure, but not the whole of it. Understand Juan José?

JUAN JOSÉ. I think so Mister Robinson. And I will try to be more super positive now.

JACKIE. That's a good deal right there son. Now look here, I want you to give my game ball to that Boy there.

> *(A boy suddenly stands up stage populating JJ's dream.)*

JUAN JOSÉ. Yes sir el Jackie…

JACKIE. Hustle up now.

> *(JUAN JOSÉ approaches the AFRICAN-AMERICAN BOY in dapper brown suit, tie and dandy fedora. He holds a yellow lemon ice.)*

JUAN JOSÉ. The Great Jackie Robinson there…

---

*Reference image can be found at: http://www.racismreview.com/blog/2011/03/11/no-dogs-or-illegals.

> (JACKIE *and The Boy share a wave and smile.*
> *Jackie exits.*)

JUAN JOSÉ. The man just tell me to give you his priceless game ball...

AFRICAN AMERICAN BOY. Neat-o. Never got one before. Thank you kindly mister.

JUAN JOSÉ. Who are you little man?

AFRICAN AMERICAN BOY. My name is Emmett Till. From Chicago Illinois I am.

JUAN JOSÉ. Emmett Till? *(heard this name before)*

EMMETT TILL. Yes sir.

> (**EMMETT** *crosses to exit and suddenly pivots with*
> *real child-like caution and a message for* **JUAN**
> **JOSÉ.**)

Be very careful out here – in the American Night.

> (*A child's warning hangs in the air and* **YOUNG**
> **EMMETT** *is gone:*)

> (*Crack of bat – Crowd cheer of woodstock!*)

> (**JUAN JOSÉ** *reads his handbook as images flood*
> *the stage:*)

> (*MLK's voice:*)

"I have a dream that my four little children will one day live in a nation..."

> (*Shotgun blast or crack of thunder and more*
> *images!*)

> (*Hear RFK:*)

"And now it's on to Chicago..."

> (*Walter Cronkite:*)

"Four dead in Ohio in what some are calling the Kent State Massacre..."

> (*Shotgun blast more crowd cheer*)

> (*Santana's soul sacrifice crashes in.*)

(**BOB DYLAN** *and Baez rise from the floor on a small stage made of a large faded Mexican Coca Cola sign.*)

(**JUAN JOSÉ** *jumps on the rising stage and grabs the MIC.*)

JUAN JOSÉ. Hello Woodstock!!!

(*Crowd roar and a lone* **WOODSTOCK HIPPY** *enters and dances all sunshine fairy stoner with crazy eyes.*)

Does anybody know how many miles to the Promised Land?

BOB & JOAN. (*singing*)
HOW MANY ROADS MUST A MAN WALK DOWN,
BEFORE YOU CALL HIM A MAN...

JUAN JOSÉ. I just hear where The Man kill the Robert Kennedy and Martin Luther, Malcolm X and all these innocent people man, it is too crazy! And right now, I have too many *pinche* questions and not enough *pinche* answers...

BOB & JOAN. (*singing*)
THE ANSWER MY FRIEND IS BLOWN'... THE ANSWER IS BLOWIN' IN THE...

JUAN JOSÉ. I am more lost than ever...

JOAN. (*light and airy*) Lost is okay man.

JUAN JOSÉ. I don't think I will make a good American. So right now, I'm going to burn my US Constitution pocket book!

(**JOAN** *has taken a super human inhale toke but still speaks:*)

JOAN. You burn that book man you burn our First Amendment, our individual right to come together and collectively express our outrage against the machine man. To question authority. Our political freedoms our civil liberties...

JOAN. They came at a cost man. And it's the most grooviest most beautiful thing about being an American. And that is why those great men died…

(She exhales finally on the final syllable.)

JUAN JOSÉ. *Me vale verga.* Maybe I just go back to Mexico!

JOAN. You wanna bum out all these people at Woodstock, man?

(The one CONCERT GUY *protests:)*

CONCERT GUY. You're bumming me out man! I'm going back to Burning Man!

(Lone CONCERT GUY *is gone.)*

JOAN. You should'a just taken that dirty money, man…

JUAN JOSÉ. What did you say? You look very much like my Lydia.

JOAN. I'm not Lydia man I am a conduit…

JUAN JOSÉ. *¿Que qué?*

BOB. She's a West Virginia Coal Miner, she's a Tambourine Man she's a Spotted Owl on *(sung)* Maggie's Farm!

JUAN JOSÉ. *¿Que qué?*

JOAN. I am a portal. A vessel. A medium with messages for Juan José…

BOB. She is the Walrus. Koo-koo cachou…

JUAN JOSÉ. God bless you, Bob.

JOAN. I have information, some useful, some not. It flows thru me to you.

JUAN JOSÉ. What kind information you have for me Walrus?

JOAN. Art school is the new law school…

JUAN JOSÉ. I don't understand…

BOB. Stay outta Cal Arts man…

JOAN. That's not cool Bob man.

BOB. I meant Sarah Lawrence man, I had a bad trip with her once!

JOAN. Bob, go wait in the corporate jet man…

BOB. Right on Joan. Shit, I wasn't even at Woodstock man. Factually incorrect *shame on the playwright!* For shame...

(**BOB** *steps off stage and shuffles over to Juan.*)

(*speak/sing Dylan songs*) *You got a lot a of nerve... There must be some kind of way outta here – said the Joker to the Thief... Who killed the Kennedys, who killed Tupac who killed Biggie Wha wha?*

(**BOB** *is face to face with* **JUAN JOSÉ.**)

Lookie here Deportee, don't forget about The Beats and Coltrane and Charlie Parker they're American too. Like an Appalachian Love Song or Friday Night prayers of the Sephardim *in* Spanish. Our contradictions and innuendo fascinate even a Wretch Like Me! It's *all* America kid!

JUAN JOSÉ. I don't understand Señor Bob Dylan.

BOB. Just remember this above all else:

America sucks, but it swallows...

JUAN JOSÉ. I will try to wrap my *cabeza* around that one Bob...

BOB. Hey there's Janice Joplin getting high with Whitney Houston and Phillip Seymore Hoffman! Too soon? Yeah... Fuck me!

(**BOB** *exits blowing his harmonica.*)

JUAN JOSÉ. America is *not* groovy funky Conduit Gwoomans!

(**JOAN** *strums her ukelele.*)

JOAN. Let me tell you about a groovy American, who like you, came to these here United States as an immigrant, he came with a wonder lust in his heart and sweat on his brow, but he *Kept on Truck'n man...*

(**JOANIE** *sings the first verse of "The Ballad of Harry Bridges."*)

(**HARRY BRIDGES** *enters through the audience shaking hands.*)

(**JOAN** *and* **MORE UNION HALL VOICES** *[recorded cast] sing the third verse of "The Ballad of Harry Bridges."**)

(*We must see images of Bloody Thursday and San Francisco Dock Worker riots. Like Manzanar they help the audience greatly.*)

(**JOAN** *descends back thru the trap in floor.*)

HARRY BRIDGES. Thank you Joanie, dear. The Occupy Movement sure could have used you! Amy Goodman wants you to ring her. Careful going down the hatch hope that's union labor down below! You *betcha*!

> (**HARRY BRIDGES** *in 1930s suit and fedora extends his sure hand.*)

JUAN JOSÉ. *Señor* Harry Bridges?

HARRY BRIDGES. (*Aussie accent sure!*) Call me Harry son. So you wanna work on the docks do you boyo? Will you stand with the Longshoreman's Union man?

JUAN JOSÉ. I think so, okay Mr. Bridges.

HARRY BRIDGES. Not *think* son that just won't do. We need your blood and guts, your brains and some muscle too. Help us organize the workers on this San Francisco Water Front and then San Pedro way.

JUAN JOSÉ. San Francisco?

> (*Distant Foghorn.*)

HARRY BRIDGES. You betcha! We're going against the company bosses son, we aim to burn the snitch books and unionize all the men. I need someone to help me organize the Spanish Sailors.

JUAN JOSÉ. I do what I can Harry. I speak the Spanish very good...

---

*Please see Music Use Note on page 3

HARRY BRIDGES. You remind me of me son. *Cuando yo era joven*, fresh off the boat I was and plenty scared they'd snatch me up and send me back to where I came from.

JUAN JOSÉ. This scare me very much too Harry Bridges.

HARRY BRIDGES. Wayfaring lads we are, but *never* afraid of sweat and toil! What skills do you possess son?

JUAN JOSÉ. If you have Spanish Influenza I can take you down to the Willows and bury you very nice next to Mister Johnson.

HARRY BRIDGES. That is quite a skill son. Ever load a ship, mate?

JUAN JOSÉ. Chip *no señor*, but I will try Harry.

HARRY BRIDGES. I'll sponsor ya, son. Let us welcome our newest union member On The Waterfront everybody! *(encouraging audience)*

MAN IN AUDIENCE. Excuse me! Hold on, excuse me, I'm sorry may I say something?

> *(A **MAN IN THE AUDIENCE** with a receding hairline and short blond ponytail walks toward the stage.)*

> *(A Goth-y put-upon stage hand hands him a microphone.)*

HARRY BRIDGES. What's on your mind brother? Speak up man...

MAN IN AUDIENCE. Thank you Harry. Yeah, right now, I'm a single mortgage payment away from losing my house. Sometimes I have to choose between Cymbalta for my wife OR food for the kids. I'm humiliated Harry. Truly humiliated.

HARRY BRIDGES. I hear you loud and clear friend.

MAN IN AUDIENCE. And then these illegal aliens keep coming here and taking away the skilled jobs from the skilled Americans...

JUAN JOSÉ. Why he so angry with me? What is this?

HARRY BRIDGES. *Your* dream just turned into a Town Hall Meeting kid.

ANGLO WOMAN IN AUDIENCE. Who wants *TEA*!?

> *(A well-dressed Audience Member with large tea bag and cup.)*

HARRY BRIDGES. Tea Baggers. Damn.

ANGLO WOMAN IN AUDIENCE. *(w/MIC)* Our emergency services are totally maxed out. *They* come in with their Mexican anchor-babies, their narco-drugs and killer brown bees and Mexican killer bees! My son was stung recently!

MAN IN AUDIENCE. They want Obama-care!

> **(ANOTHER MAN** *wears work clothes and ball cap with a blond wig.)*

ANOTHER MAN IN AUDIENCE. Send them back!

ALL. Send them back! Send them back!

HARRY BRIDGES. Send them back you say?

ALL. Yeah! Send them back!

HARRY BRIDGES. If we sent everybody in this room back to where they came from, every last one of you would be sitting in a foreign country...

ANOTHER MAN IN AUDIENCE. Ah come on Harry!

HARRY BRIDGES. *(pointing at audience)* It's true! Germany, Israel, Poland, Phoenix Arizona...

JUAN JOSÉ. *(to audience member)* That guy is from Fontana I think...

HARRY BRIDGES. Let me handle this son.

JUAN JOSÉ. Si Harry...

HARRY BRIDGES. He only wants a job good citizens!

MAN IN AUDIENCE. I want a job too! But that don't mean I stand around the Home Depot like a pack of wild wolves, urinating on the sidewalk in a Bart Simpson T-shirt that says Cowabungu dude!

ANGLO WOMAN IN AUDIENCE. English only please.

MAN IN AUDIENCE. Of course. My bad.

ANGLO WOMAN IN AUDIENCE. He's a gang-banger! Clearly…

ANOTHER MAN IN AUDIENCE. Wake up America god dammit! Wake up.

MAN IN AUDIENCE. We need to secure our borders with *armed* citizens!

HARRY BRIDGES. Bring back the armed citizen militias you say?

ANGLO WOMAN IN AUDIENCE. We have a very nice militia here in Lancaster…

ANOTHER MAN IN AUDIENCE. Harry, I belong to A Benevolent Armed Militia Pride Cooperative in Malibu Canyon – Adjacent – we are – Thee Vigilant Honey Badgers… Many of our senior members are in the audience here this evening and I'll tell you what Harry, we're *scurred* man we're *tared* and we want America back!

HARRY BRIDGES. Yes I have heard that…

ANOTHER MAN IN AUDIENCE. And I want my foreskin back, Harry.

HARRY BRIDGES. I'm so sorry…

ANOTHER MAN IN AUDIENCE. Cheap Mexican labor hurts American Unions Harry!

HARRY BRIDGES. Now there's a hard fact. Get me Tom Hayden on the line!

ANOTHER MAN IN AUDIENCE. *Barack Obama is coming for our guns!*

> (*He pulls a firing pistol and fires several rounds.*)

Don't worry it *is* not loaded…

> (*Pow pow pow! Gun is fired.*)

HARRY BRIDGES. Put that firearm down, man!

ANGLO WOMAN IN AUDIENCE. He has a right to bare arms!

> (*Man with gun lights up a huge vapor cigarette.*)

MAN IN AUDIENCE. But *no* smoking pal!

ANOTHER MAN IN AUDIENCE. Can I keep my gun?

MAN IN AUDIENCE. Sure, but *no* vapor smoking!

HARRY BRIDGES. Are we not a country built by and for immigrants?

ANGLO WOMAN IN AUDIENCE. That was a long time ago pal.

HARRY BRIDGES. Look man, the FBI tried to deport me several times...

AUDIENCE MEMBERS. FBI?! Whoa...

HARRY BRIDGES. That's right. Because I was an immigrant, an immigrant who stood up to the greedy bosses and the thugs who refused to give a man a decent wage.

> *(Town Hall Grumbles)*

HARRY BRIDGES. An injury to JUAN is an injury to all!

ANGLO WOMAN IN AUDIENCE. Ouch. Hey Harry Bridges is an Extreme Community Organizer!

AUDIENCE MEMBERS. He's a Communist *and* a bad poet. He's a Jewish person I know it! Close the borders! Close the borders! Close the borders!

> *(A Middle Eastern Woman steps to the stage from the audience.)*
>
> *(She is articulate, soft spoken and a young University Student.)*
>
> *(She wears a HIJAB, skinny black jeans and a fitted black radiohead T-shirt with the word "creep" on it.)*

YOUNG HIJAB. Have we become a nation of bullies?

> *(Town Hall people stop for a moment. Taken aback by the HIJAB.)*

Unable or unwilling to take on the *real* bullies?

ANOTHER MAN IN AUDIENCE. OH MY GOD Al Qaeda woman! *(pointing in hushed man-horror)*

ANGLO WOMAN IN AUDIENCE. What are you saying young lady?

YOUNG HIJAB. "Give me your tired, your poor, your huddled masses...?"

ANGLO WOMAN IN AUDIENCE. Oh speak English!

YOUNG HIJAB. Shall we load Mexicans on box-cars and ship them back after we're done with their cheap labor?

HARRY BRIDGES. Not another Bracero program, *NO!*

ANGLO WOMAN IN AUDIENCE. Why don't you go back to where you came from!

YOUNG HIJAB. I just drove in from the Loyola Marymount campus.

ANOTHER MAN IN AUDIENCE. *(with a cough to cover not so well)* Liberal Lesbian Catholic Arts College... Um...

MAN IN AUDIENCE. After thirty-five years of dedicated service to my company they just fired me man... I'm rendered obsolete!

ANOTHER MAN IN AUDIENCE. Guys like us – middle aged white guys – we are expendable man.

YOUNG HIJAB. There is trauma for both colonizer and colonized perhaps?

ANOTHER MAN IN AUDIENCE. Ya think? *(truly uncertain)*

HARRY BRIDGES. Nobody is expendable or obsolete. What is your work friend?

MAN IN AUDIENCE. I.T.

JUAN JOSÉ. Aye Tea?

HARRY BRIDGES. *(to* JUAN JOSÉ*)* And did *this* man take your job?

MAN IN AUDIENCE. No sir. HE DID!!!

(A young ASIAN MAN *in the audience stands up:)*

ASIAN MAN. Don't point the finger at me just because I'm Asian!

ANGLO WOMAN IN AUDIENCE. Go back to where you came from!

ASIAN MAN. Fine. Send me back to Stanford and I'll get my *second* degree! And I will bury because I am more educated than you, I work faster and I take less time off and I'm skinnier. *Biatch!*

ANGLO WOMAN IN AUDIENCE. Watch your language, you Oriental asshole!

ASIAN MAN. Supply and demand sugar tits...

ALL. Get rid of the Orientals! Send back the Orientals!

AFRICAN AMERICAN AUDIENCE MEMBER 1. May I say something please? May I say something please?

> *(A well dressed **AFRICAN-AMERICAN MAN** is walking to stage.)*

MAN IN AUDIENCE. Oh great, the soft-spoken black guy. I'm outta here!

HARRY BRIDGES. Let the man speak. Please sir, go right on ahead...

AFRICAN AMERICAN MALE AUDIENCE MEMBER. Thank you Mr. Dundee. Look, I have lived in a working class mostly black neighborhood in Seattle my entire life. Many of our folks were lucky enough to have started out in the shipping yards there.

HARRY BRIDGES. Long live the Local 19!

> *(With a hard athletic and inappropriate slap on the buttock.)*

AFRICAN AMERICAN MALE AUDIENCE MEMBER. That was awkward. Look, we held those good Union jobs for years until those jobs up and went away. Then all the foreigners started moving in and it pushed the Black Folk out of the black neighborhoods. I have a sister in LA and she says the same thing is going on down there too *garsh darn* it...

ANGLO WOMAN IN AUDIENCE. Lets watch that language Kanye West!

AFRICAN AMERICAN FEMALE AUDIENCE MEMBER. South Central ain't even black anymore! It is infested with the Salvadorans and Mexicans and Guatemalans and whatnot...

JUAN JOSÉ. *Pero mi casa es tu casa...?!*

AFRICAN AMERICAN AUDIENCE MEMBER 2. My *casa* is *not* your *casa*, baby! *(fussing with her M Obama bangs!)*

ANGLO WOMAN IN AUDIENCE. We need Arizona Sheriff Joe Arpaio!

YOUNG HIJAB. Okay. Let's take a closer look at Arizona Sheriff Joe Arpaio then shall we?

> (**SHERIFF JOE** *hits the runway with a driving techno beat.*)

Himself, the son of hard working Italian immigrants who settled in the state of Massachusetts after Liberty Island.

> (**SHERIFF JOE** *is working the beat like a male club whore. *Crucial given the techno music and hijinks of the club whore* **SHERIFF** *that* **YOUNG HIJAB** *truly prosecute her case for* **JJ***!*)

Decades later Sheriff Joe *remakes* himself into a Western style sheriff complete with cowboy hat, holster, badge and loaded six-shooter. Our kind Sheriff is "reborn" the good guy. Juan José the bad and the ugly. Why were Sheriff Joe's immigrant parents allowed to find sanctuary in America but not others?

HARRY BRIDGES. *Híjole* she's good mate!

YOUNG HIJAB. Allow Juan José to remake himself as Sheriff Joe has.

> (**JUAN JOSÉ** *alone applauds.*)

SHERIFF JOE. Can I see your papers young-lady?

YOUNG HIJAB. I was born in America...

SHERIFF JOE. Your papers Taliban Girl!

ANGLO WOMAN IN AUDIENCE. Let's see Obama's papers!

AFRICAN-AMERICAN MALE AUDIENCE MEMBER. Hold on now...

AFRICAN-AMERICAN FEMALE AUDIENCE MEMBER 2. Please don't go there! Hold my earrings somebody!

> (**AFRICAN AMERICAN WOMAN** *removes her hoop ear-rings and steps to* **ANGLO AUDIENCE WOMAN** *who gets mari-macha bravo [brave] with her swinging purse as they are pulled apart.*)

SHERIFF JOE. *(to* **JUAN JOSÉ***)* Young man, I need you to step over here.

> (JJ *moves toward the* **SHERIFF** *as the fighting Ladies chill.*)

Did you attempt to buy a piñata earlier today?

JUAN JOSÉ. For my son *yes.*

SHERIFF JOE. Here's what we're gonna do for you, we're going to arrest you so turn around place and your hands behind your wetback.

HARRY BRIDGES. On what charges are you arresting this good man?

SHERIFF JOE. Attempted Piñata buying is suspicious criminal activity in the state of Arizona...

YOUNG HIJAB. How is this *not* racial profiling?

AFRICAN AMERICAN FEMALE AUDIENCE MEMBER. It's a post-racial world baby!

YOUNG HIJAB. *(quietly)* Not in Ferguson Missouri... Not for thousands of immigrants detained in desert detention centers.

JUAN JOSÉ. Obama Manzanar? *(to himself and truly confused)*

ANGLO WOMAN IN AUDIENCE. What are you saying young lady?

YOUNG HIJAB. I think we may have a morality issue here...

ANGLO WOMAN IN AUDIENCE. What are you saying?

YOUNG HIJAB. I think we may have a morality issue here...

ANGLO WOMAN IN AUDIENCE. How dare you. I am a Christian.

YOUNG HIJAB. *(earnestly yearning to know)* Then where is our Christian Charity?

ANGLO WOMAN IN AUDIENCE. *(coy)* In Israel with Glenn Beck and the evangelical hard-liners?

YOUNG HIJAB. Are we *all* God's creatures or just some of us?

ANGLO WOMAN IN AUDIENCE. I'm very okay with just some of us.

HARRY BRIDGES. Holy be-Jesus... *(under breath)*

YOUNG HIJAB. Jesus! Okay, he is walking in the desert:

> *(Techno music blasts! hits the center runway like fire.)*

He's coming toward you, you see him, he's filthy, he's dark, his accent is thick like smoke, he's wearing some hot sequence and in terrible need. Do you give Jesus water? Would you give an animal water? Or do you arrest Jesus?

> **(JESUS** *stops dancing and lays a hand on* **JJ***'s forehead and another hand to the heavens as* **JJ** *has bowed to him.)*

SHERIFF JOE. Okay let me see you papers Hay-soos.

> **(JESUS** *checks his robe but cannot produce his papers.)*

Let me see your hands pal.

> **(JESUS** *obliges holding palms up outstretched for inspection.)*

Stigmata. Good to go!

> **(JESUS** *jumps for joy and exits but not before a cell phone picture with the giddy* **AFRICAN AMERICAN WOMAN.** *Picture flash!)*

AFRICAN AMERICAN FEMALE AUDIENCE MEMBER. *Thank* you Jesus!!!

ASIAN MAN. *(from audience)* Hey I just got a text message: I just got fired from Google!

AFRICAN AMERICAN MALE AUDIENCE MEMBER. Welcome to my world. *Biatch*!

ASIAN MAN. *(reading)* I'm unemployed because of an I.T. guy in *India?*

> **(INDIAN MAN** *in orange turban appears in upstage door.)*

MAN IN TURBAN. *(reasonable accent)* Oversees outsourcing mother-fuckers!

HARRY BRIDGES. *(grim)* America is on a Swift Boat to Mumbai!

AFRICAN AMERICAN FEMALE AUDIENCE MEMBER. It's all them Mexican's fault!

JUAN JOSÉ. Mister Bridges? *Por favor!*

> *(Town hall folk make their way toward a worried* **JUAN JOSÉ.***)*

ASIAN MAN JOINED BY ALL. Get the Mexican! Get the Mexican! Get the Mexican!

JUAN JOSÉ. *Ayúdame Harry!*

HARRY BRIDGES. This would be a *very* good time to speak English Juan José…

ALL. *Send them back. Send them back. Way back!*

JUAN JOSÉ. But I am legal!

ALL. Harry! Harry! Harry!

> *(Town hall Crowd is turning into a and now wearing blue windbreakers with ice on the back in huge yellow letters: Immigration and Customs Enforcement.)*

> *(They close in on* **JUAN JOSÉ** *making tribal-like sounds and stylized circular dance movements. rejoins them:)*

MOB. *(calm-like-then-building)*

Hooga-booga-hooga-booga, send them all back.

JUAN JOSÉ. I promise to be a good American!

MOB. *Hooga-booga-hooga-booga.* Ashes, ashes, all fall down!

> *(The Vanilla Ice mega-hit song slams in like a mother-fucker.*)*

> *(sings)*

ICE ICE BABY! ICE ICE BABY! ICE ICE BABY!

---

*Please see Music Use Note on page 3

(The **MOB** *dance morphs into the* **ELECTRIC SLIDE** *line dance.)*

*(***MOB***/dancers hoist* **JUAN JOSÉ** *as* **JESUS** *blesses him:)*

JESUS. *En el nombre del Padre y Hijo y Spíritu Santo...*

JUAN JOSÉ. I want to go home Mister Bridges!

HARRY BRIDGES. Keep your wits about you son! Grace kid!

JUAN JOSÉ. I will try Harry I will try! I don't think I can make it!

HARRY BRIDGES. I am your life-coach and I say you can son!

JUAN JOSÉ. Maybe you are wrong Harry Bridges...

HARRY BRIDGES. Stay on the bloody trail son!

JUAN JOSÉ. The Bloody-Bloody Trail Harry?

HARRY BRIDGES. No matter. Right smart son!

*(***HARRY BRIDGES*** *is gone.)*

JUAN JOSÉ. No leave me Harry. Everybody hates me!

YOUNG HIJAB. I don't hate you Juan José!

JUAN JOSÉ. Arab-Spring Lydia-Esperanza!?

(She fades away and exits as:)

(A super energetic **JAPANESE GAME SHOW HOST** *enters!)*

GAME SHOW HOST. Who wants to pray "Who Wants to Be An American!!??

MOB AUDIENCE. *He* does!

(The **MOB** *places* **JUAN JOSÉ** *down, runs off screaming.)*

(The stage becomes a "Who Wants To Be A Whatever..." like TV set with moving shafts of light and spinning doors and lights.)

GAME SHOW HOST. Juan José! You are almost home. Almost off the Lewis and Clark, Latter Day, Mexican Trail! For very special chance to take short cut across bloody trail to USA Citizenship, I ask you: are you ready to pray "Who Want to Be American" Juan Jose-san?

JUAN JOSÉ. Eh…

(Dramatic millionaire like music blast: Tan tan tan…)

GAME SHOW HOST. Okay Juan José, I will call you JJ – JJ! You are three questions away from winning your American Citizenship – If you lose – you'll be sent back to Mexico wearing this exploding whitey-tight-y under-wear!

(A spokes-model languid from Japanese fatigue and a heavy blonde wig enters in gaudy red dress holding fully rigged explosive whitey-tight-y briefs with lit sparklers.)

Holy Mexican *terrorista!* Shabu. Shabu! Please answer correctly so we don't blow up! Okay. Let's pray! Your remaining categories JJ are: Jerry McGuire, Black Snake Moan or United States History!

JUAN JOSÉ. I take US History!

GAME SHOW HOST. Excellent choice JJ-san! Okay, please listen most carefully: what famous American was first Postmaster General who also create American Library and was author of "Poor Richard's Almanac"? Quiet audience! Warning. Let JJ think…

JUAN JOSÉ. First US Post Office worker?

GAME SHOW HOST. Your answer JJ!

JUAN JOSÉ. Señor Benjamin Franklin – final answer!

(Upstage door opens to reveal Benjamin Franklin in period dress with a flying kite. ([layed by African American Female track])

BEN FRANKLIN. You know dat's right boyee!

(A Lightning strikes the kite. Explosion.)

Yeah baby!!! *(aroused and satisfied)*

GAME SHOW HOST. Next question… Listen very carefully JJ: Name acquisition of land by United States from the

Frenchie. Very large territory also include two Canadian provinces: Alberta *and* Saskatchewan.

JUAN JOSÉ. I think I need subtitles because I can barely understand you.

GAME SHOW HOST. Very funny!!!

(*A flash of raw sashimi anger then composure –*)

Acquisition of land JJ. C'mon! Audience I warn you do NOT answer for JJ. If you do, you will have to wrestle this large SUMO wrestler!

(*A larger* **SUMO WRESTLER** *with shiny man-tassels stomps on.*)

SUMO. Wasabi, Teriyaki, Sake... Kim Chi Taco Truck!

GAME SHOW HOST. Juan José, answer please. Hay!

JUAN JOSÉ. The, Louisiana Purchase. Final answer!

GAME SHOW HOST. Ha! *Correcto!!!*

(*Music and lights accents and stabs.*)

Final question standing between JJ and official US Citizenship Documentation!

(*We see a large US social security placard with* **JJ** *'s face.*)

Super-Grande question for JJ-san. Everything on line for you. All the marbles. Okay. Name the three branches of the United States Government?

(**SUMO WRESTLER** *warns audience not to answer! Clicking clock.*)

Name three branches of USA Government...

(*Clock tics. Mounting tension.*)

I sink you know this one JJ... C'mon. Sink JJ, sink!

(*All grows silent save for tension music.*)

Does JJ want Lifeline? (*tension*) Audience wait with great anticipation JJ. Just name three branches son...

JUAN JOSÉ. Yes. No. Stop the music!

GAME SHOW HOST. But Citizenship is so close for JJ!

JUAN JOSÉ. I really don't want to play this game anymore…
America, is kind of a *loco* place for me. I want to go
home now. Please?

GAME SHOW HOST. Silly JJ, you *have* no home…

> (**GAME SHOW HOSTESS** *laughs vacant like a
> Warhol Chelsea Girl.*)

SUMO WRESTLER. He no answer. What do we do now boss?

GAME SHOW HOST. JJ must do honorable thing:

ALL. *HARE KARI*!!!

> (*Huge knife is provided. Explosion. All rush* **JUAN
> JOSÉ**.)

> (*Lights and sound send* **JUAN JOSÉ** *into a tight
> whirlwind as the and* **GAME SHOW HOSTESS** *help
> strip* **JUAN JOSÉ** *of some of his clothes.*)

> (*In the chaos a life raft tracks or traps up center
> stage.*)

> (*Sounds transition to that of the ocean. In a
> moment:*)

> (**JUAN JOSÉ** *alone in a raft on the flotsam of the
> ocean.*)

> (*Projected infinite ocean/water horizon line.*)

> (*A blue wash and pin spot for* **JJ** *– Radio Static
> then:*)

SOOTHING NPR FEMALE RADIO VOICE. All seven youths
were acquitted today in the November 2008 Long
Island stabbing death of Marcelo Lucero, in what
prosecutors claim was an ongoing campaign of terror
targeting Hispanic MALES. The accused Teens actively
participated in "Mexican hopping" throughout Long
Island…

> (*Radio dial and static catches random airwave
> snippets:*)

CUBAN RADIO VOICE. Radio Mambi! It's eighty-five degrees in Hialejia and ninety degrees en *Calle Ocho*! *Attention!* A Cuban man left Havana several days ago.
Coast Guard officials confirm the lone survivor is drifting somewhere in the shark-infested waters of the Atlantic... May god save his soul and Death to Fidel! And now we return to Rush Lim...

> (**CELIA CRUZ** – *Salsa Queen enters in huge wig and fabulous gown.*)

CELIA CRUZ. Azúcar! Honey! I am Celia Cruz. ¡*Azúcar*! Be careful *nene*, no *jodas* baby! ¡*Azúcar*!

> (*Two vegas style back up dancers with sequence shark heads follow Celia in a salsa line and dance to her mega hit: "Carnival."*)

Look out for the Charks Juan Jose! The Charks honey!

HIPSTER SHARKS. Charlie don't surf!!!

> (*Enter* **ABRAHAM LINCOLN** *with top hat and tails and a golden Oscar.*)

JUAN JOSÉ. Señor Abraham Lincoln?

LINCOLN. Won't you join Mrs. Lincoln and I in the balcony Juan Jose?

> (*Enter a young* **AFRICAN AMERICAN MAN** *in Statue of Liberty foam costume and twirling a large sign that reads immigration lawyer and cash for gold and classes on how to Lose Your Accent!*)

Greetings and felicitations my Good Negro, you are a Free Man now!

FOAM BROTHER. Uh... Okay. Thanks. Juan Jose, stay out of the balcony AND grad-school man!

JUAN JOSÉ. What is grad school man?

FOAM BROTHER. Bunch of bullshit is what it is!

> (*Enter* **JUAN JOSÉ**'s *father from Mexico with cowboy hat and boots.*)

JUAN JOSE THE 2ND. So you are a Dreamer now *eh cabrón?* Your American Dream?

JUAN JOSÉ. Papa?

JUAN JOSÉ THE 2ND. Why are you drifting alone in the Pacific Ocean *hijo de puta? ¡Contéstame pinche morro!* You bring shame to the entire country of Mexico! You break your mama's heart. You leave your wife and baby behind! What kind of man pledges his allegiance to a new land that does not want him? Even liberal gringos don't want you here *cabrón!*

(*Pointing to audience.*)

The rumors back home! They say that you are gluten free and that you teach Pilates and have the Gringo ADD and OCD and bi-polar curiosities and quite possibly LGBT-QA. Now I am going to whip you in front of these very well dressed subscribers!

(*Papa smiles and waives to the Gringos and whips* **JUAN JOSÉ:**)

Puto!

JUAN JOSÉ. *Ay!*

(*Gregorian Chants as a hooded Franciscan Monk crosses up stage.*)

JUAN JOSÉ THE 2ND. (*with a whip*) Wake up the Angle of Death is here!

(**SKINNY TIE'S # 1 AND 2** *from before appear. Father stomps off.*)

SKINNY TIE # 2. Get thee behind me Satan!

JUAN JOSE THE 2ND. *¡Chinga su madre!*

SKINNY TIE # 1. Juan José, Juan José!

JUAN JOSÉ. Joseph Smith, Brigham Young? Brother Lewis and Clark?

SKINNY TIE # 1. We are here amigo to save your soul!

SKINNY TIE # 2. In the Waters of the Latter Day Saints we baptize thee…

JUAN JOSÉ. In The Gulf Stream Waters?

SKINNY TIE 2. Cool your brow in thy crude oil...

(They dump black oil water on him.)

JUAN JOSÉ. Wait! Wait!

SKINNY TIE # 1. Do you feel the Holy Ghost JUAN JOSE?

(This could be a baptism or water torture just as:)

SKINNY TIE # 2. You are reborn! *(then both rejoice)* Hallelujah Juan José!

*(3 **SECT WOMEN** in bonnets, and colorful dresses enter like ballerinas with big gulp drinks and straws. Angel Voices Sing:)*

ALL SECT WOMEN. *(angelic voices)*
    HAL—LE—LU-YAH...

SECT WOMAN 1. Husband?

SECT WOMAN 2. Husband?

SECT WOMAN 3. Husband?

JUAN JOSÉ. I am all your husbands? I am Ladder Day Saints?

*(**SECT WOMEN** slurp from the Big Gulps as if to answer "yes". Sound of low flying helicopter and **FBI VOICE** on bullhorn.)*

FBI VOICE. Your religious compound is surrounded!

*(We hear "Flight of The Valkyries." **SECT WOMEN** scramble panicked.)*

There is no escape Juan José. Release your twenty-five wives and two hundred illegitimate immigrant anchor babies or else: *Achy Break-y Heart!*

*(The chaotic sounds mix and crescendo with The Valkyries, Helicopter, a Ships Horn and screaming **SECT WOMEN**.)*

*(One of **SECT WOMEN** Brides rolls across the stage like a human tumbleweed or Isadora Duncan dancer from the Helicopter force.)*

*(**LYDIA**'s voice echoes in the swirl of chaos:)*

ROW ROW ROW YOUR BOAT, GENTLY DOWN THE STREAM,
MERRILY MERRILY MERRILY, LIFE IS BUT A DREAM...

> *(Then suddenly silence:)*

> *(JJ is utterly alone. He weeps in his lonely raft a broken man.)*

> *(A door opens or descending from above revealing:)*

> *(Sound of ocean – a lonely gull:)*

LYDIA. Husband?

JUAN JOSÉ. *Lydia... Mi amor?*

LYDIA. What are you doing there now husband?

JUAN JOSÉ. I am drifting in the ocean. Never arriving. Never existing...

LYDIA. Our son is one year today.

JUAN JOSÉ. *Dios mio... (realizing that a year has passed)*

LYDIA. You have been gone too long husband. A baby needs to hear his *papá's* voice... He must have this...

JUAN JOSÉ. I leave that world for this one, but now I lose my way in the Valley of the Shadow of the Sonoran Dessert...

LYDIA. Did you ask Saint Anthony for help?

JUAN JOSÉ. I forget to do this *mi amor...*

LYDIA. *(spoken) Dear Saint Anthony please come around, my husband is lost and cannot be found...*

JUAN JOSÉ. Tell my boy *papá* love him so...and I am sorry...

LYDIA. This make me very sad... Where's all your stuff?

JUAN JOSÉ. Lost. Or gave it away I don't remember...

LYDIA. You have nothing again? You could have stayed *here* for that.

JUAN JOSÉ. But you *must* remember, you were at the police station *mi vida*, you told me to *take* the cartel money!

LYDIA. I say we *need* the money, I never say *take* it. *Semantics.*

JUAN JOSÉ. You are true *mi amor...*

LYDIA. What kind of place is over there? America. It is good?

JUAN JOSÉ. They kill a man on Long Island today. They kill him because he *was* an immigrant. He will sleep tight? His American Night.

LYDIA. My goodness… You have melancholy I have not heard before…

JUAN JOSÉ. Yes *mi amor*. The lonely ocean is crushing my bones.

LYDIA. You *will* find a safe place for us.

JUAN JOSÉ. I have no more *Esperanza*. Please tell my boy:
Balas y Besos. (Bullets and Kisses)
Sustos y suenos… (Frights and Dreams)

LYDIA. I make a song for you so you can find your way back to The Road…

> (**LYDIA** *deftly whips her ukulele from around her back.**)

> (*It is okay too if the audience finds the whipping around of the UKE humorous for it will fight against our enemy: Sentimentality.*)

> (**LYDIA** *sings "Tongiht You Belong to Me" un-adorned. She heard it on the radio once coming from the US to her little Mexican Pueblo.*)

> (*Characters from earlier in the Play/Journey slowly re-enter as* **LYDIA** *ends the final verse of the song.*)

> (**LYDIA** *vanishes behind closing walls.*)

> (**JUAN JOSÉ** *rises out of the raft with the help of his Great-Grandfather The Mexican Revolutionary from West Texas.*)

JUAN JOSE THE FIRST. *(private)* Tú eres hombre de valor/You are a man of valor…

---

*There is an un-sentimental Mexican sensibility at work here, the idea of: "If there is trouble, then I will sing!"

(**HARRY BRIDGES** *enters and tosses a towel* −)

(**JOHNNY** *from* **MANZANAR** *offers a his comb on a Pachuco chain* −)

(**MRS. FINNEY** *offers a clean and pressed Shirt* −)

(**JACKIE ROBINSON** *has an old Brooklyn Dodger Jacket* −)

(**VIOLA** *enters with her bottle and a teaspoon of Castor Oil.*)

VIOLA. *(private words)* Make Viola and your son proud...

(*The raft disappears into the floor.*)

(*All recede into the shadows in the wings except* **JUAN JOSÉ**...)

(*The buzz of the alarm clock radio shatters the silence.*)

(*Harsh light and the stern Female* **VOICE:**)

VOICE. Your citizenship test begins now.

JUAN JOSÉ. *Bueno.*

THE VOICE. Name the three branches of the US Government?

JUAN JOSÉ. The Executive. The Legislative and the Judicial.

(*Time and sound lapses forward:*)

VOICE. Your final question: name the Original Thirteen Colonies.

(**JUAN JOSÉ** *clears his throat. Beat.*)

Name the Thirteen Colonies...

JUAN JOSÉ. *(deep breath)* I *need*... I *want* to answer this important question. *Okay*...

(**JUAN JOSÉ** *hears an echo of his own Ballad:*)

New Hampshire. Massachusetts. Rhode Island.
Connecticut. *(breath)* Delaware.
Nueva York, New York − New Yersey.
Pennsylvania.

North and South Carolina...
Virginia.
Maryland *y la* Georgia.

> (*He raises his arms for a moment of triumph and smile.*)

Eso sí... I did it!

> (*He then realizes he must go back for his family and the daunting task ahead. Slowly fade to black as we hear:*)

I did it...

> (*Lights continue to dim on our American Knight in silence.*)

> (*In black we hear the opining dramatic strains of* **NEIL DIAMOND**'s *"They're Coming to America."**)

> (*Entire Cast quickly marches on stage joining* **JUAN JOSÉ** *as:*)

NEIL DIAMOND. Congratulations Juan Jose, you are a new American!

Welcome to the 99 percent! Let's Occupy America tonight goddammit!

> (*Cast including the Exalted Cyclops of the KKK begin to dance.*)

> (**NEIL DIAMOND** *sings a parody of "They're Coming to America." For the original lyrics, please contact the playwright, Richard Montoya, via email at rjmon59@gmail.com. Producing organizations can also create their own parody. However, copyright restrictions still apply, as detailed in the Music Use Note on page 3.*)

> (*At song's end* **JUAN JOSÉ** *re-emerges with wife and baby car seat.*)

> (*Our New American Family restored!*)

---

*Please see Music Use Note on page 3.

ALL.

THEY'RE COMING TO AMERICA –
THEY'RE COMING TO AMERICA – TODAY! TODAY!

(All strike the "today" with triumphant fists in the air!)

(Curtain call proper / Cast bow.)

(Led Zeppelen's "Immigrant Song" is walk out music!*)

(Fin.)

---

* Please see Music Use Note on page 3